GOLDEN ROSE

KENYA STEMMONS

KANSAS STREET PUBLISHING

CONTENTS

DEDICATION

I dedicate my first novel to the little girl who didn't have a voice. I see you and I am your protector.

PREFACE

The title Golden Rose derives from the premise that nothing can stop a rose from growing, not even hardened concrete. My motivation for writing this book is to delve into the complexities of mother-daughter relationships and how this formative relationship may influence every relationship thereafter.

As I wrote this book, it started to serve as my own therapeutic outlet to analyze my complex relationship with my mother and how it has a life of its own and influences my relationships, past and present. As I grew older, I realized that my mother taught me not only what she knew, but also what her mother taught her about being a woman. It is my hope that through this novel, women will gain an introspective look at their own relationships with their mothers and how this formative relationship colors all others.

Golden Rose is a coming-of-age story of a twenty-five-year-old named Golden who attempts to unearth her own identity separate from the gritty world she grew up in. She is met with ups and downs: some of these as the consequences of her choices and some as those of choices made before she was born.

The mother-daughter theme in this novel is explored through the trials and lives of three generations of women. Golden Rose centers around the belief that the older generation's values and ideologies (good or bad) are passed down from one daughter to the next until someone decides to break the chains of poverty, drugs, abuse, and self-loathing to create a new future of their own design.

In this novel, it is the youngest of the three generations, Golden, who has the courage to step outside the dead-end life laid before her by her mother, Althea, and her grandmother, Mother Rose. These three generations of women are a product of their harsh environment. So please, do not judge them too harshly.

Step into the world of these three women chronicling the influences of one generation upon the next and how they weave and intertwine into one another. Step inside the world of Golden Rose as she attempts to maneuver through life with the collective experiences of her elders. Will these experiences help Golden in dire times or will her ancestral experiences usher in her ultimate demise?

Chapter One

THE CLANK

Golden hated coming here. The long drive, going through security, so many eyes watching her with distrust. She hated having to stuff packs of cigarettes in her panties for Mother Rose. Golden's mother, Althea, always ran through the routine with her before they walked through the barbed-wire gates.

"Make sure you don't fidget, or somebody may think you got something going on." Althea motioned with her eyes toward Golden's groin. "Now, remember as soon as you go in, hug Mother Rose then go over to the toys and place the squares under the red bucket. You got that?"

"Yes, Momma, I got it," Golden replied in her small voice. Golden was more concerned with showing off her black-and-white polka-dot dress she had helped design than the task at hand: smuggling cigarettes into a federal prison.

Golden jumped at the loud sound of the buzzer that let the inmates know visitation started. The inmates rolled in, some slowly and some hurriedly, scanning the room for their loved ones. Althea quickly walked toward the visiting table nearest the play area, pushing past anyone meandering aimlessly. She had to get the table closest to the play area because Golden might drop the pack of cigarettes.

Mother Rose was incarcerated for getting caught with thousands of dollars of stolen designer clothing. Mother Rose had made a career of stealing and scamming. She never wanted to work an hourly wage: there wasn't enough money, plus, an hourly job could not keep pace with Mother Rose's extravagant lifestyle. After six years of fraudulent activity— that the Feds were aware of—she was finally caught on camera stealing from a high-end department store. The Feds now had sufficient evidence to connect her to a string of unsolved retail theft crimes. The Feds got lucky and were able to flip a coconspirator. One of Mother Rose's regular customers in conjunction with wire transfers and fraud revealed Mother Rose bought social security numbers from a connect she had at the social security office. Her connect would give Mother Rose social security numbers of babies as soon as a request was initiated at the hospital. By the time the parents realized the child's social security number was compromised and their identity stolen, it was almost impossible to prove when the security breech had happened. Oftentimes, the parents were blamed because they could not prove they weren't involved. Mother Rose usually had about ten years with the social security numbers before she would stop using them. This crime was the most lucrative scam of Mother Rose's criminal career. She even sold some of the social security numbers to other people she knew, and they used them to illegally obtain credit cards and loans and to send fraudulent wire transfers.

Mother Rose raised Althea to believe this type of criminal lifestyle was normal. She shunned other parents who struggled to feed their families from nine-to-five jobs. Mother Rose gossiped about secretaries and garbagemen in their neighborhood, belittling them in front of Althea.

"Look at they dumb ass, working all them hours for the man and still ain't got shit" Mother Rose would say. She believed in living moment to moment with no concern for the future.

Even though Mother Rose was incarcerated, she convinced Althea to continue to fuel her need for status. But the only people Mother Rose had to impress were her fellow inmates. Mother Rose was known for having the latest fashion, hair, and makeup. She had no plans of prison stopping her from continuing to keep up a front. But that cost money, and Mother Rose only had one outlet to make money: her daughter, Althea. Mother Rose convinced Althea to smuggle contraband into the prison for her to sell to other inmates. If Mother Rose had things to sell, then she had power, and with power came money and respect. Mother Rose's newest hustle was selling cigarettes and a few pre-rolled joints to the inmates.

On a routine collect phone call Mother Rose bullied Althea into another one of her schemes. "I need you to do something for me, gal. These chimney sweepers getting dirty in here," Althea whispered into the community phone.

Althea already knew what that meant. She'd seen Mother Rose in jail more times than she could count, but it became increasingly difficult to smuggle things to her over the years because Mother Rose was serving time at prisons that had tighter security due to the nature of her crimes. Althea knew that Mother Rose didn't care about her risks. She simply expected Althea to submit to her demands.

"Get that lil' dumb tar baby to help you," Mother Rose added, referring to Althea's daughter, Golden.

Mother Rose always spoke down to Althea about Golden because she still resented Althea for forgetting about her when she fell in love with Diamond, got pregnant with Golden, and moved out. So, Althea felt eternally guilty for leaving Mother Rose and spent her adult life indebted and subservient to her own mother. Mother Rose knew this and played on Althea's guilt.

Althea thought of a plan to smuggle cigarettes into Mother Rose so she could use them to barter and control other inmates. Althea tried to smuggle in some weed too, but she ended up smoking it instead to calm her nerves before driving to the prison to visit Mother Rose. Althea physically shook the idea out of her head about how upset Mother Rose would be knowing she wouldn't be delivering the other part of her prison order. She knew Mother Rose was going to insult her for smoking the marijuana instead of bringing it to sell. Althea resolved to herself, "Oh well, what she gonna do, whoop me?" She shook her head, sat up straight, and rolled back her shoulders, attempting to project strength.

Althea and Golden made the long drive to the Federal prison. Althea hated the drive. She gripped the steering wheel so hard the two-and-a-half hours that by the time she made it to the prison parking lot her shoulders were in knots and her hands cramped. Althea found a parking spot far from the other cars and against the fence. She always parked here because the shade from the trees obscured the view of the cameras that surrounded the prison and parking lot. Althea needed the coverage to place the packs of cigarettes into Golden's panties. The guards usually used only the wand on children and rarely did a pat-down. Althea gave Golden "the speech" before they went inside the prison.

"Now remember, don't do all that moving around. As soon as we get there, you go over to the play area and put the squares underneath the red bucket. Now repeat it back to me, what color bucket?" Althea quizzed Golden. Althea was satisfied that her daughter understood what to do, so they got out of the car and made their way to the visitor's entrance. Althea liked to arrive early so they would be able to get to the table nearest the play area first, but that meant standing in line longer than the rest of the visitors. She knew this was risky because Golden would get fidgety and impatient. Today, however, the doors to the visitor's entrance opened earlier than usual.She took it as a good sign.

Golden and she went through security. Althea broke into a cold sweat but tried to remain cool. She had to snatch Golden's arm a few times to stop her from scratching her panty line.

"But it itches, Momma," Golden whispered loudly, causing a guard to eye them suspiciously. Althea's breath caught in her throat; she feared they were caught but the guard waved them into the long hallway leading to the visitor's room. The pair quickly entered the room and headed straightaway to the table nearest the play area.

Just then, Mother Rose made her way to the table from the other side of the room and grinned widely showing her glittering smile decorated by two fanged gold-teeth. She walked slowly, clocking the guards posted at each corner of the room and in the visiting room control tower. She carefully sat next to Althea with her back to the play area so she could easily view any curious eyes. If an inmate or visitor looked too long in her direction, Mother Rose would stare at them and cock her head to one side as they uncomfortably redirected their gaze elsewhere. Mother Rose quickly shifted her eyes to the side, motioning Althea to tell Golden to go to the play area and plant the three packs of cigarettes in their usual hiding place.

"Mother Rose," Golden said. "You see my new dress? I helped design it with Grandma."

Before Mother Rose could answer, Golden stood and twirled and jumped around in a circle with glee for Mother Rose to get a better look at her custom black-and-white polka-dot dress. Before Golden could catch it, a pack of cigarettes popped out of the band of Golden's panties and fell on the floor with a plop that echoed across the room on the grey, stained floor. The sound of the pack of cigarettes falling reverberated against the concrete walls and floor of the visiting room. Some of the inmates' eyes fixated on the pack of cigarettes that had fallen from Golden's dress. "Uh oh," Golden said and froze mid-twirl.

"Inmate!" One of the guards yelled as he thudded across the room in his orthopedic shoes, also noticing the pack of cigarettes.

"You stupid motherfucker!" Mother Rose loudly hissed at Golden. "What the fuck? What the fuck you do? Damn, don't nobody care about that little dumb ass dress!"

Mother Rose began to stand with her hands outstretched toward Golden's tiny throat.

As the guard approached Mother Rose, another guard made a straight line for Mother Rose as well and started to bring out her handcuffs.

"Man, I knew yo' dumb ass was gonna fuck up," Mother Rose yelled at Golden mid-lunge, but by this time both guards reached Mother Rose and started to restrain her, which only made her angrier because she couldn't get to Golden.

The guards had to use all their strength to restrain Mother Rose by slamming her face on the table in front of Althea. An inmate at the next table, seeing an opportunity to apprehend the unattended pack of cigarettes, foolishly lunged from her seat onto the floor. Another guard in the observation room saw the commotion and quickly hit a button indicating an immediate lock down, letting off a loud siren that blared from all corners of the visiting room. Another security guard left his post from one of the corners of the visitation room and grappled with the inmate who had picked up the cigarettes. In the commotion, the guard stomped the pack of cigarettes to bits of tobacco, filter, and paper while putting the inmate in handcuffs. Pandemonium ensued among the inmates and visitors because they knew their visits were being cut short due to the trio of Mother Rose, Althea, and Golden.

Chaos erupted in the visitation room as Mother Rose struggled against the force of the guards and let loose an onslaught of unthinkable insults against Althea and Golden. One inmate yelled, "See, that's why I can't stand that bitch, she think she better than everybody!" More guards rushed into the visitation room to restore order.

"Inmates, down on the ground! Lockdown!" A guard yelled over the PA system. "All visitors make your way to the exit, visiting hours are now over."

Shouts of anger, cursing, crying, and yelling comingled with the Golden's tears. She didn't understand why Mother Rose and everyone else were yelling at her, while her mother, Althea, sat frozen in her seat. She was so still that Golden became frightened.

"Don't bring yo ass back here, motherfucker! And take that dumb ass, black ass baby with you!" Mother Rose yelled over her shoulder as she was dragged out of the visiting room by two guards on each side.

Althea quickly grabbed Golden and hurried to the exit. She tried to push her way into the confusion of the crowd, but a guard effortlessly grabbed them both by their collars, choking them and stopping their advance. The guard quickly spun both around and held them with his large hands underneath their armpits so they couldn't move. The guard ushered them into a tiny room, closing the door behind him and making the room soundproof. All the protests and cries from the inmates and visitors instantly stopped, and the pair was surrounded by an eerie quiet. The room was stuffy and no bigger than a broom closet, with only a light and a floor drain.

Golden was still sobbing. "I'm sorry, Mommy...I'm sorry, I can do it right this time. I'm sorry." Golden pleaded to Althea, holding and yanking her hand with both of hers, tears streaming down her small face.

The pair stayed locked in the small room for what seemed like an eternity to Golden. Then another guard came in, completely filling the doorway with his body so that only his silhouette was seen. "You are no longer allowed in any other Federal Bureau of Prison facilities. Do you understand?" The guard bellowed in a deep voice, awaiting a response from Althea.

Althea, head hung, nodded in acknowledgement, never meeting eyes with the guard. "You know, we can have your daughter taken away and put in the system for this stunt you pulled today, don't you? What were you thinking?" the guard asked Althea in a sincere tone. His voice was so full of concern that it made Althea immediately feel ashamed.

She was ashamed she was in a broom closet with her daughter at a federal prison. She was ashamed she even let Mother Rose talk her into smuggling cigarettes into the prison. Most of all, Althea was ashamed she couldn't say no to Mother Rose.

Althea broke down sobbing. "I'm sorry, I'm sorry, I know, I know." Her hazel eyes met the gaze of her daughter's eyes, red with tears. It was the first time Althea looked at Golden since they were locked in the room. Althea let out a sob from the pits of her diaphragm. Althea saw her own face reflected in the eyes of her child, begging for understanding, begging for love and acceptance. Althea didn't have the words to explain what just happened, and she let out another guttural sob.

The guard filled his chest with air and let it go loudly. "Look, I had a momma just like that. I used to get into all types of bullshit behind her! But I had to wizen up and leave her ass in the past. You young... got your whole life ahead of you. You got your own daughter to think about. What happens if she get taken away, huh?" The guard paused, took in a deep breath, then let it out. "I know her daddy gone."

Althea's eyes quickly shifted to the guard questioningly. Her thoughts began to fill with thoughts of Diamond. She would never be here visiting Mother Rose if he were still alive. They would be long gone from this small city and living out their dreams like they planned.

"You knew Diamond?" Althea asked the guard in a whisper.

"Look, everybody in the hood knew Diamond and what happened to him. Ya'll was hood celebrities. Damn shame what happened." The guard paused, exhaled again. "Why you think I'm here?" he asked. "The game changed after he left. Had to get me a job, provide for my family. When Diamond left, the money dried up. We all had to find another way, but this right here ain't it. He wouldn't want you up here with his baby on this bullshit!" The guard shifted his weight to his other foot in his big, black work boots. "Look, I'm gonna let ya'll go, off GP. Don't bring yo' ass back up here. Ya' hear?" The guard paused and waited for Althea to indicate her understanding.

"Thank you," Althea replied, nodding in gratitude.

Althea wiped the snot from her nose with her sleeve. The guard stepped to the side, freeing up the doorway as light flooded into the tiny room with redemption. The guard personally walked Althea and Golden through every security door and gate in the prison, all the way to their car. Althea and Golden rode in silence the whole two-and-a-half-hour ride home.

Golden pretended to be asleep in the back seat to avoid the piercing stares of her mother in the rearview mirror. She always knew when Althea was angry because her eye color changed from light hazel to muted emerald, the same color as Golden's eyes.

Golden felt the familiar turns of the car as they made their way back into the city and then their neighborhood. She began to relax as she felt the car make a right turn onto Kansas Street. She knew her grandmother would be sitting on the couch, eagerly awaiting their arrival and news of Mother Rose's reaction to the dress Golden sewed and created primarily on her own. Golden tensed at the thought of the day's events. She reluctantly got out of the back seat and heavily headed up the stairs to their house at a safe distance behind Althea.

The door creaked open, and Golden saw her grandmother sitting on the couch with a half-smile playing on her lips as she knitted. "There's food on the stove, Thea. How was ya'll's visit?"

"Ask yo' granddaughter," Althea spit out.

Golden's grandmother slowly put down her knitting needles, her eyes shifting back and forth from Althea to Golden. "What happened, Thea? Golden?" Neither of them answered.

Golden couldn't hold back her tears any longer and started to sob again. "S...sh..she...hated it," Golden stammered.

"She...who...hated what...what happened?" Grandmother looked confusingly from Golden to Althea.

"Gone 'head and tell her, Golden. Tell her what happened." Althea walked to the kitchen, slamming her purse on the table.

"I...I...I didn't mean to," Golden couldn't stop sobbing. "I j..jj...j ust wanted her to see my dress."

Grandma got up from the couch, which took some effort, and went into the kitchen to face Althea. "Now, what happened?" Grandma asked in a cool, even-toned voice. She needed answers.

"She went up there and embarrassed us all." Althea let out a breath seemingly held all the way from the prison and fell into a heap in the nearest kitchen chair. "She was so happy about that damn dress, them damn cigarettes fell outta her panties and everybody saw! We almost got arrested!" Althea folded her arms across her chest. "Could've lost her," she said, her voice lowering to a whisper. "Now we can't ever go back there."

Grandmother looked from Golden to Althea in disbelief. She was trying to process the story. She couldn't believe Althea tried to sneak cigarettes into the jailhouse for that no-good Mother Rose!

"Well," Grandma said in an even tone. "I'm just glad ya'll home safe." She gave a warm smile in Golden's direction. "Baby, go on in there and wash yo' face and hands so you can eat." Grandma watched after Golden until she slowly gathered herself and turned toward the bathroom. Grandmother wanted to make sure Golden was safely out of hearing range before she spoke again to Althea.

Grandmother slowly walked to the stove to ensure the food was cooking evenly and not burning. She wiped her hands on a kitchen towel and sat next to Althea. Grandmother stared at Althea while trying to choose her words wisely.

"Thea, now I came down here when you first got pregnant because my grandson asked me to help out with you and the baby and ya'll family. Then when he got murdered." The words got caught in Grandmother's throat and she paused. "I decided to stay 'cuz I knew you didn't have no help. Yo' mama never gave a damn 'bout Golden, or you for that matter." Grandmother paused because she knew what she had to say would hurt Althea, but she cared more about Golden's feelings.

"Now what did I tell you when I decided to stay after my grandson was killed?" Grandmother waited patiently for an answer from Althea.

"You told me you would stay as long as I put Golden first," Althea replied flatly.

"You know what I meant by that?"

Althea finally looked up at Grandmother with tears streaming down her face. "I said that with Mother Rose in mind. That woman only cares about herself and herself alone, and you know that! You been trying to earn that woman's love since you came out the womb, but a woman like that is incapable, baby! She just can't do it! But that's yo' momma and you can't help but love her. Just like that baby in there can't help but to love you, no matter how wrong you do her." Grandmother paused and reached out to turn Althea's face toward hers. "As long as I'm alive I will protect that baby and I'll do whatever I have to do. You understand?" Grandmother held Althea's chin and gazed into Althea's eyes until she nodded with understanding. "Now lemme fix you a plate and you go lay down, I'm sure you're tired from your journey." Grandmother began to hum "At the Cross" while she fixed Althea's plate.

Meanwhile, Golden was standing in the bathroom, trying to wrap her young mind around the day's events. Her head felt heavy and her nose raw from the combination of crying and wiping. She looked in the bathroom mirror at her reflection and all she could see was the black-and-white polka dots on her dress staring back at her. The white collar of her dress was hanging on one end where it was ripped from the guard grabbing her. Golden furiously clawed at her collar, ripping it from the rest of the dress. She tugged at the fabric, recalling all the horrible things Mother Rose said in the visiting room. She remembered all the angry visitors and inmates screaming at her, and she felt like the walls were closing in. Her vision started getting fuzzy around the edges. She felt like the dress was choking her and if she didn't get it off immediately, she didn't know what would happen Golden stripped down to her panties, fell to the floor in a ball, and hugged her knees. She rested her head on her knees as she began to sob, but her eyes couldn't produce any more tears. Then she smelled a hint of tobacco lingering from the cigarettes and emitting from her panties. So, she got in the shower and scrubbed the day away and threw her beautiful polka-dot dress in the bathroom garbage.

Golden awoke in her bed. She was disoriented as the door of her bedroom creaked open and Grandmother's sweet smiled appeared, which instantly comforted her. Grandmother came in her room carrying a plate and a cup. Grandmother sat on the edge of Golden's bed while she sat up and scooted over to make room.

"Here baby, I know you hungry, so I heated up your plate and brought yo' favorite red Kool-Aid." Grandmother handed Golden the cup, which she greedily gulped. Grandmother gently took the cup and placed Golden's plate of food on her lap and lovingly watched as she slowly ate.

"I set up a surprise for you, but I reckon you didn't even notice." Grandmother turned her head toward a corner in the room. Golden craned her neck to look around Grandmother to see a desk with a lamp on it that cast a pale-yellow hue over the room. Golden was confused because the desk wasn't there this morning, and she couldn't remember if she saw it before she laid down. Golden looked at Grandmother with a questioning look.

"Go on over and see," Grandmother urged.

Golden peeled back her covers and slowly walked over to her new desk and her eyes widened in the darkness, attempting to adjust to the dimly lit room. As she got closer to the desk, she saw some of the fashion sketches she had created over the last few months. She didn't know Grandmother was collecting them. She noticed an organizer with sketching and colored pencils. There was also a black, leather book laying on the desk with gold-embossed lettering that read "Golden." She gently traced the letters with her fingers.

"Go on, open it!" Grandmother urged.

Golden opened the cover and inside there was a note scribbled in Grandmother's unmistakable small handwriting. Golden leaned in close to read the note.

Always be you, you are the master of your destiny. No one else.

"It's a sketch book for all of your fashion ideas," Grandmother said sweetly as Golden read the note in her head.

Golden closed the cover of the book and began to trace the embossed letters of her name again with her finger.

"Sit down baby," Grandmother gently guided Golden back over to her bed. "You know I knew you were special the day you came into this world. We all did, yo' daddy included," she paused. "Yo' momma wanted to name you something else like Keisha or Tanisha. But yo' daddy took one look at your beautiful dark skin and green eyes and said your name was gonna be Golden because your skin was so dark it glowed." Grandmother smiled at the memory. "He loved you so much, baby. You gotta know that. He gave you that name because he knew you were special, and I know it too."

Golden sat on her bed and hung her head, thinking about Grandmother's words and the thought of her dad. Moments passed and Golden lifted her eyes to meet her grandmother's.

"I miss him so much," Golden admitted. "I wish he was still here."

"Me too baby, but life goes on. I don't want you to get so wrapped up in the sorrows of yesterday that you forget the joy of today."

Golden gave Grandmother a puzzled look. She always had a way with words that Golden didn't understand at the time but always made sense later. She waited for Grandmother's explanation.

"I know earlier today Mother Rose and ya' momma said some not-so-nice things to you, but I don't want that to keep you from what makes you happy."

Grandmother busied her hands with fabric in her lap. Golden realized it was her tattered black-and-white polka-dot dress. Grandmother had rescued the dress from the bathroom trash.

A moment of silence passed, and Golden became embarrassed because Grandmother found the dress. Golden pressed her lips together tightly, fighting back tears. She didn't want Grandmother mad at her too.

Grandmother sensed Golden's tears. "I'm not mad baby, I just don't understand. You were so happy and proud of yourself for designing and sewing this dress. Remember when we went to the fabric store and the joy you felt when you saw the exact fabric you sketched?"

Golden nodded her head and felt a flicker of happiness, recalling her feeling in the fabric store. It was like her vision coming to life right off the page. She remembered how it felt working side-by-side with Grandmother, sewing her creation. Then she quickly felt the pang of disappointment as she recalled the prison scene.

Grandmother sensed the shift in Golden's mood. "See...that right there?"

Golden was snatched out of her thoughts.

"That's what you don't do, you don't think about somebody else's reaction to what you do. You focus on how your work makes you feel." She grabbed Golden's hands and placed them on the fabric. "You remember how you felt when you bought this fabric, right?"

Golden blinked her eyes.

"Well, that's the feeling you stay with. Your own feelings. People gonna come and go, but don't give them power over how you feel about yourself. You understand?"

Golden nodded. She didn't really understand all that Grandmother was saying, but her words did remind her of the joy she felt when she saw the fabric in the store for the first time. She decided to never let anyone steal her light ever again.

"And as far as Mother Rose goes, you ain't ever gotta see her again if you don't want to. Sometimes the family you born with ain't the family you stay with." Grandmother always had a way of simplifying the world for Golden.

No one ever spoke of that day again, and that was the last time Golden ever saw Mother Rose.

Chapter Two

EMERALD STALLION

Golden grew into an exquisite young woman. She looked like a runway model gracing the catwalks of Paris and Milan. Golden Rose stood about five ten with a slender, athletic frame. Her skin resembled the most exquisite Brazilian coffee bean of a deep chocolate brown. Golden had the type of body women would pay for and men lusted after. Her full C-cup breasts sat perky on her chest, melting into her delicate shoulders that highlighted her clavicle. Her elongated neck seemed to go on for days, leading to her small chin and pouty lips. Her nose was small, but rounded at the tip, guiding to her haunting eyes. Her eyes were the color of fall when green started to fade from the earth, pale and signifying the changes in season. Hints of gold flecks in made her eyes even more mesmerizing against the canvas of her perfectly dark, coffee-bean skin tone.

Golden's green eyes were inherited from her mother, Althea, who always boasted about her daughter's eyes. However, when Golden was born, there were no hints of green in her eyes; they were light hazel, hence, her name, Golden. When her mother and father stared at her, they saw the perfect blend of their features in their beautiful daughter. As Golden turned one, flecks of green began to come to the forefront of her irises. Not many people could stare Golden directly in her eyes for long before her beauty caused intimidation and self-consciousness. Men were enchanted by Golden, and she knew the power her beauty held over them. Her mother taught her how to use her beauty to her advantage and how to manipulate men to get what she wanted by selling them a fantasy. Golden was especially equipped for selling a fantasy to older men who had passed the prime of their glory days. They knew it and so did Golden. She gave them the attention only a young, vibrant woman could give a man in the throes of a mid-life crisis: attention that stroked his failing ego and sexual prowess.

Golden had little time for love. She was taught that love makes you weak and only brings you sadness. She watched her mother seduce men who came to court her after her father died. These men would come to the door with the guise of "wanting to check on Althea and Diamond's seed." But these men had ill intentions. Althea was a hood celebrity growing up. She turned down almost every guy in high school, but when Diamond came along, she couldn't resist and fell deep in love. When Diamond was killed, the vultures set in, circling Althea, waiting for any sign of weakness so they could finally feast upon her flesh. As they watched Golden grow into a beautiful woman, those same men that lusted after her mother also lusted for Golden as well.

In the early days after Diamond's death, Golden would watch from her secret hiding place between the couch and the side table as her mother answered the door to gentleman callers. Althea would ask who was at the door before she opened it. Who was on the other side of the door determined the character Althea played. She would either mess her hair up to look grief-stricken, or she would quickly get her robe out of the closet closest to the door, take off her shirt, and adjust her breasts so they would topple and jiggle in her bra. She made sure she looked fetching using the mirror on the inside of the closet. If Althea was really interested in the gentleman, she would stick her thigh out slightly from behind the folds of her robe. She could play the role of the grieving widow or the sex kitten, depending on the man and the wad of cash in their pocket.

Golden watched this scene play out repeatedly throughout her childhood until the steady stream of men stopped coming on a regular basis. Maybe word had gotten out around town that Althea was a tease and she wasn't going to have sex with any of the men. In Golden's teenage years, she started to notice a different type of man coming to the door for Althea, smelling of cheap alcohol, weed, and stale cigarettes. These were the men Althea would leave the house with and return, sometimes the next day, stumbling drunk and passing out on the couch, unconscious for hours. Golden would lean down and press her face to her mother's just to make sure Althea was still breathing.

Sometimes Althea would spend the next three or four days drunk and high, depending on who she was spending time with. Sometimes, Althea would come home with wads of cash. Golden began to get smart and would steal money out of her mother's purse to buy food and pay the utilities for the household. As a teenager, Golden knew how to call and get extensions on the utilities because her mother was absent mentally and physically. The only bright spot in Golden's everyday life was the presence of her grandmother.

Grandmother came to live with Althea and Diamond when Althea was pregnant with Golden. Grandmother was more like a mother to Golden since Althea was so young and unequipped to raise a child. Grandmother brought calm and organization to an otherwise chaotic environment. Grandmother always encouraged Golden to follow her dreams of being a fashion designer. In fact, Grandmother was the first person to invest in Golden by buying her sketch table and her first sewing machine. Grandmother also showed Golden how to use her sewing machine and to pattern her designs.

Grandmother told Golden how beautiful she was each day before Golden left the house. Golden modeled her self-styled looks every morning before school for Grandmother's approval. Sometimes Grandmother would give suggestions for Golden to try a different accessory, but that was rare. Usually, Grandmother simple smiled and nodded at Golden, saying, "You look beautiful, baby." And that nod of approval was all that Golden needed to go out and face the hardships of the day.

Grandmother always said, "A woman should always look good because if you look good, you feel good. You gotta keep your hair and nails done and never let yourself go." Golden lived by those words. She styled her clothes, hair, nails, and accessories to convey her mood to the world. If she wore a high twenty-four-inch ponytail with a leather dress and studded heels, that meant she felt like a bad-bitch and nobody better get in her way! Golden perfected her looks in high school and on into her career as a manager at the mall.

Golden was obsessed with fashion. She knew all the names of the fashion houses and their origins. She also studied fashion trends based on decades because she knew that fashion repeated itself. She wanted to stay abreast of current fashions and attempt to predict new trends. Her fashion predictions were based on spring and fall fashion shows from all over the world, but her favorite were from Italian designers. She loved how the femininity of the clothing didn't take away from the strength of the woman wearing it.

She loved creating quick sketches of her outfit before going to bed, which included her desired hairstyle and accessories to complement her outfit of the day. She also created makeup looks to accompany her clothes and complete her fashion story. Golden really got to shine at work. The more outrageous her makeup, the more products she sold at her makeup counter. Women in their teens and twenties were all trying to become the next social media influencer, and they came to Golden's makeup counter for inspiration. Oftentimes, Golden rocked her signature clothing pieces to work, sold directly off her body for the right price! Her store manager frowned upon the practice but let Golden have a pass because she consistently brought in the highest number of sales each week.

Golden knew her sewing skills were not perfect. However, she knew they were good enough to sell to her small customer base. Golden calculated that if one of her pieces held a customer's gaze for more than five seconds, then she had a winning piece and possible sale. If her piece did not hold a woman's gaze or gain a compliment, then she knew she had to go back to the drawing board. She wasn't worried about the men looking because they always looked; they couldn't help but be drawn to her unique beauty.

"I can't wait to move outta this town," Golden complained to her favorite sales associate. "I'm gonna save my money, go to fashion school, and never come the fuck back!"

"Oh, so you finally applied, did you?" Gerald asked her in a condescending tone. He already knew the answer. Golden always talked about going to fashion school but never completed and turned in the application. "I didn't think so," Gerald whipped his head around and his body followed.

Golden always saw her herself moving out of the Midwest to a big city where she would make her mark on the fashion world, so she knew it was important to figure out who her customer was. What fabrics they liked and what colors and patterns they were drawn to. She didn't feel confident in her work just yet. She repeatedly told herself, "I'm gonna get just a little better at sewing, then I'mma apply to fashion school."

"Anyway, bitch, you just jealous 'cuz these hoes ask about me when I ain't here and you can't make a sale without me." Golden gave a smirk and walked to the other side of the makeup counter to finish stocking the understock beneath the display cases. She knew that comment would irritate Gerald. Her thoughts were confirmed as she heard him slamming boxes behind her.

"Damn, bitch! Don't break the powders." Golden burst out laughing. Gerald tried to stifle his laugh, too, but he joined Golden's irresistible laugh. In all the years they worked together, he could never stay mad at her long.

"I can't stand you, hoe," Gerald replied and gave an imaginary swat in Golden's direction. The two continued to work in peace.

"But for real though, Gerald, you think I'm good enough to go to school?" Golden turned toward Gerald with a sincere look on her face.

Gerald whipped his body around to quickly join Golden at the other side of the makeup counter. "Hell yeah! You one of the most talented bitches I know! You can sell snow to a snowman and these heifers stay coming in her jacking yo' style. So why shouldn't you go to school?" Gerald asked Golden and waited for an answer.

"You know I can't leave my grandmother," Golden whimpered.

"Mmkay, Golden, whatever you say. Your grandmamma wants you to go, too, so don't put her in it." Gerald paused and walked away from Golden. "And you know I'm right. If you scared G, just say you scared."

Golden didn't reply and continued to work in silence for the remainder of her shift.

The only person who truly understood Golden's love for sewing and designing was Grandmother. In fact, the only person who made Golden feel as though her dreams were obtainable and not far-fetched was Grandmother. She always asked, "Goldie, baby, you design anything new this week? I sho liked that other design."

Golden would smile and answer *yes* or *no,* and then Grandmother would encourage her to get out her sketch pad while Grandmother sat and watched her create. It was their special time where all else ceased to exist. There was no sense of failure for not attending fashion school. There was no shame of having a self-absorbed and abusive mother. She wasn't the child of a slain drug dealer. She was just her grandmother's baby.

Grandmother knew Golden needed confidence if she were ever going to break free from Althea's looming shadow. Grandmother understood that Althea had given up her dreams of happiness long ago when her grandson died. Althea was scared to live, but that didn't have to be her Goldie's fate. So, Grandmother encouraged Golden at every opportunity. Be it though a new fabric, trim, or embellishment Grandmother brought home. Golden was always surprised to come home to the gifts that would help her craft laid out on her tiny work desk in her room. Golden oftentimes wondered how Grandmother afforded all her gifts, but Grandmother always explained it best, "the Lord provides ways to grow our gifts."

CHAPTER THREE

PIPE DREAMS

Golden started her day the same as always: mindlessly scrolling through all her social media to see if she missed anything while she was asleep. Her socials focused on beauty brands, fashion, modeling, and photography. She picked out her outfit of the day. She was inspired by '90s pop music that day. So, she dug in her closet and broke out her blue-and-grey plaid miniskirt and a white collared shirt paired with a navy blue cardigan. She finished her outfit with iconic black Mary Janes and white knee socks. She didn't feel like looking innocent that day, so instead of ponytails, she wore her sleek, jet-black wig that was parted down the middle and cascaded down her back. She added a few gold broaches with chains and different colored stones to her cardigan to complete her look. She added a bright orange blush to accent her dark skin and high cheekbones. She decided on a clear, super glossy lip and extra-long lashes that looked like those of a baby doll. She looked in the mirror and blew herself a kiss.

Golden exited her room and was greeted by the disheveled image of her mother sprawled out on the couch in a matted wig, and her salmon-colored bathrobe with a black cotton teddy underneath. Golden took a deep breath, and she crossed the room to the front door. Golden placed one hand on the handle, stopped, and turned her head to stare at her mother in disgust and pity. The entire living room smelled of cheap vodka and stale cigarettes. Golden thought for a split second, "just die," as she stared at her mother's legs sprawled apart as if her gentleman caller had just climbed off and left. Golden was immediately so ashamed of the wish for her mother to die that she released the door handle, walking over to Althea who was lying in a heap on the couch.

Althea's body was motionless. Golden coughed to get her mother to move, but Althea was unresponsive. "Ma!" Golden yelled. Still no movement. "Ma! Momma!" Still no movement from Althea.

Golden stepped closer to look for the rise and fall of her mother's chest, but there wasn't any movement. Golden, now horrified, immediately threw down her purse and began to violently shake Althea's shoulders. "Ma...Ma...wake up...Ma...Mommy!" Golden begged. Althea opened her eyes with a snarl on her face.

"Get yo' damn hands off me, dammit!" Althea had a crazed look in her eyes, and her breath smelled metallic and sick. "You always looking all sorry. Well, I ain't dead yet. And where you going? Looking like a fake Britney," Althea's words shredded into Golden.

"I gotta go to work," Golden spat out. But before she stood all the way up, Althea grabbed her forearm and held on tight.

With a smirk on her face, Althea said, "Oh so what, you going to the mall to impress them white folks? They don't care about you. You think you cute, don't cha?" Althea tightened her grip. "Well, you ain't shit, girl! You hear me...you ain't shit. Little Ms. Uppity think she's better than everyone," Althea hissed. "Well, why you still here if you better than all us? Huh?

"You think somebody gonna come and look at those little sketches of yours? You think you gonna get on TV and make it big? Just like yo' daddy with them pipe dreams. Well, let me tell you, ain't no fairy godmother and ain't nobody coming to save you!" Althea's words became more poisonous by the minute, making Golden regret she woke up. Then Althea delivered words that felt like a knife.

"You gonna leave me just like he did. Won't you? Won't you!" Althea now screamed. "You gonna leave me," Althea repeated until she fell into a sob and let her head hit the arm of the couch.

Golden jerked her arm away from Althea and stood up. "I'm gonna be late."

As Golden walked away, she heard Althea call after her. "Bring me some cigarettes on your way home, I'm almost out."

Golden rushed through the house, flew out the front door, and slammed the screen door behind her, fighting back tears of anger. *I wish she would've just died*, Golden thought. The tears started streamed down her face as she thought about how easily her mother angered her. Golden quickly reached in her work bag and got her compact out to fix her makeup.

Still pretty, she thought as she looked at the redness that started to form around her green eyes. She was happy about her foresight to wear waterproof mascara that day.

Golden took a deep breath and gathered herself until she felt eyes on her. She looked up from her compact and saw Marquez staring at her from across the street. She almost didn't see him because he was motionless on his porch. She didn't have time to talk to him, so she rushed to get into her car, pretending not to see him. Too late. She heard, "Hey Golden...good morning."

Marquez's voice was soothing and deep, and it sounded and felt like home. Golden couldn't be rude to him. She'd known Marquez practically all her life; they grew up across the street from each other. Marquez worked as a mechanic and lived with his mother. It was just them two since his younger brother was killed in a car accident. Marquez always had a gentle way about him and never wanted anything from Golden but for her to be happy. Golden saw him as a nuisance. Golden slept with Marquez whenever she had a breakup or just needed to feel the closeness of a man. Not to mention, Marquez was fine and sexy as hell!

"Hey Marc, gotta get to work. I'll see you later when I get off." Golden knew that was a lie when she said it. She hated the way Marquez smelled after a day at the auto garage; his skin and hair permeated with a mix of motor oil and gas fumes. But when he cleaned up, there wasn't a man more attractive that Marquez.

Golden didn't wait for a reply and got into her car, started it, and backed out of her driveway so fast her bumper hit the street with a thud. She checked her rearview mirror to see Marquez looking after her with his mouth wide open and his hand up as if he still had more to say. He looked disappointed as he turned and begrudgingly climbed the steps to his house.

Golden only lived fifteen minutes from the mall, so it was convenient for her when she had to open the store. Golden loved the mall early in the morning because it was quiet and peaceful. She always got there a little early so she could take her time and look at the new displays in the other stores' windows. That's how she stayed abreast of the newest fashion trends.

After Golden finished rounds of her favorite stores, she made her way down a single corridor leading to the back entrance of her store. Golden clocked in and spoke to the few employees that were already there. She went straight to her counter and began to clean and set up for the day. As she worked, her mother's words still rang in her head.

"You gonna leave me just like he did. Won't you?"

She didn't know if her mother meant that she was going to die like her father or she was just going to leave. Golden had to shake this thought out of her mind. She got a chill that gave her goosebumps as she thought about her father and how he was killed at twenty-five, the same age she was turning soon. A few months ago, Golden began having an eerie feeling that something big was coming. Everything that happened to her and every word that was directed her way made Golden overanalyze its meaning.

Golden tried to push the sting of her mother's words and her father's memory to the back of her mind. Work was a great distraction, and she welcomed it. Soon customers would be filling the makeup counter and Golden would be too busy to even think about her mother or her looming twenty-fifth birthday. Golden inserted her earbuds, cranked the volume, and began vibing to her favorite rap song. As she listened to the beat drop, her quarrel with her mother faded into the background along with all the other toxic conversations she had had with her mother over the years.

CHAPTER FOUR

THE INTRODUCTION

I t was a typical day at the makeup counter. Golden's favorite coworker and friend, Gerald, finally arrived. Gerald was a diva who loved makeup and was out! Loud and proud! He could make a woman's makeup look so flawless that she didn't recognize herself. All the older women went to Gerald for makeup advice and tips to make their crow's-feet and fine lines melt away. Golden, on the other hand, catered to the younger women and teens coming into the mall in search of the latest trends in makeup. They were a powerful team. Golden loved having him around because he reminded her to pursue her dreams of going to fashion school.

"Hey Gerald, I'm taking my fifteen."

While she was on break, one of the store managers called to ask if Golden could work a double shift that day because one of the other girls called off. Golden agreed because she needed the money. She still wanted to save for fashion school even if she didn't have the courage to apply.

It was late in the evening and most of the Saturday shoppers were already gone. Late night was when the mall crowd got interesting. This was the time when all the people who slept throughout the day visited the mall. The clubgoers came to find pieces to complete their look for the night. Golden decided to do inventory to make it easier for herself and her team at the end of the month. As she worked, someone behind her whispered, "Excuse me, can I get some help?"

Golden turned around to find one of the most beautiful women staring at her from across the makeup counter. She wore a black, fitted jogging suit that was unzipped so that her workout bra unapologetically displayed her abs. The woman's dark hair hung past her in soft waves. Golden was taken aback by the woman's beauty. So, Golden took a deep breath and exhaled to compose herself.

"Yes, how can I help you?" Golden asked in what she hoped was a cool, even tone.

"I was wondering if I could have my makeup done," said the young woman.

"Oh, sure." Golden smiled with a reply. "What kind of look are you going for?"

"Well, I have a gig tonight and I need a look that's gonna pop on stage," the young woman replied, lowering her head, raising her brow, and giving a knowing look. "I'm headlining at The V tonight," the woman said slowly so Golden could understand that she needed a certain look.

Golden was familiar with doing makeup for girls at The V, especially when they were starting out and didn't yet have an established onstage persona. It was a well-known fact at The V that if you needed your makeup done and you were in a bind, Golden was the go-to makeup artist. Plus, they only had to pay her twenty-five dollars at the mall makeup counter, whereas if Golden came to the club, she would charge a hundred dollars an hour and twenty-five dollars for each additional half-hour for touch-ups.

"I heard you do really great makeup," the young woman said.

"I do," Golden replied with a cocky smile playing on her lips. "Have a seat. What look are you going for tonight? What's the color of your outfit?"

"My first outfit is navy blue with navy blue sequins, but my look has to be off the chain since I'm the headliner. Sampson said he's never paid a girl how much he's gonna pay me tonight, so I have to look the part, ya' know."

Golden nodded in agreement. She had the perfect look she wanted to try on someone, but no one wore theatrical makeup in the city she lived in. So, Golden was excited to have the opportunity to create something uniquely beautiful. Since her canvas was already stunning without makeup, she already knew the woman would be jaw-dropping gorgeous when Golden got through waving her fairy wand all over her face.

"Well, let's get started," Golden said with a smile and grabbed her apron full of clean brushes. She placed a cape on the young woman to catch any loose makeup. Workers at the other counters began to eye Golden because they knew she was about to get to work, and they were eager to see how she was going to transform this beautiful creature.

"My name is Golden, what's your name?" Golden asked as she began prepping the woman's skin.

The beautiful woman raised an eyebrow when she heard Golden's name.

So, this is the makeup artist Sampson told her to come and see, the young woman thought.

Sampson urged her to go to the mall and see the green-eyed girl at the first makeup counter, but she thought for sure she would find a tall blonde with green eyes. To her curious surprise, she found a slender chocolate woman with green eyes instead. The young woman suspiciously eyed Golden and introduced herself. "My name is Tatiana, but everyone calls me Tati."

"Okay, Tati. Nice to meet you. Sit back and relax, I got you girl! Wait until they see you tonight! The men ain't gonna know what hit them, and them bitches are gonna be mad and jealous too."

Golden let out a laugh that relaxed both of them. They both knew the women working at The V would be envious because the young woman was a beautiful, young stranger. And if anything made more money at The V, it was a new face.

Golden envisioned Tatiana on stage with her hair flowing and ass bouncing to the bass with money falling around her. Golden wanted to make all the girls at The V regret not hiring her to do their makeup and only coming to the mall to short-change her and devalue her skills. The girls at The V were the main reason Golden stopped working nights at the mall. She grew tired of giving glam looks to the girls of The V for twenty-five dollars with the purchase of a product of twenty dollars or more. The girls refused to invite Golden to The V to do their makeup because they were too cheap to hire Golden at her flat rate of a hundred dollars. So, she got smart and requested a schedule change.

Golden created a navy smoky eye on Tatiana with navy and dark purple jewels on her eyelids, heavy liner, and beautiful wispy lashes. Then she created a soft dewy glow on Tatiana's already perfect olive-toned skin. As Golden worked on Tatiana, they got to know one another and quickly developed a budding friendship. It was much easier for two beautiful women to get along, Golden thought, because there wasn't any competition between the two of them. But Tatiana did appear to have what Golden was missing: money...real money.

Golden couldn't help but notice Tatiana's Rolex which was understated, but still beautiful. Tatiana wore real diamond earrings with three matching diamond-studded bracelets. Golden guessed they were at least two carats. She learned how to spot the real from the fake—especially when it came to jewelry, shoes, clothes, and handbags—from working around the real thing at the mall for years.

Golden's favorite part of creating a new look for a customer was the reveal: waiting until the end to show her customer their finished look. The way her customer's eyes grew wide as they saw themselves as beautiful as they'd ever been. Golden completed her finishing touches to Tatiana's makeup just as the mall was about to close. She handed Tatiana a hand mirror and waited for her reaction. Tatiana looked at her makeup and raised one eye. "I'll buy the lip gloss and lipstick you used, and it's twenty-five dollars for the makeup, right?" Tatiana asked in a monotone voice and dug her credit card out of her purse.

"Ummm...okay," Golden stuttered. The two women remained silent while Golden packaged Tatiana's purchases. Golden was so confused by Tatiana's lackluster reaction to her makeup that Golden spent almost an hour and a half on. Golden was fuming. She handed Tatiana her bag and wished her a good evening.

Tatiana flipped her hair and turned to walk away, then she stopped and whirled back around as Golden began cleaning up for the night. "Hey, Golden, right?"

Tatiana knew good and well that was Golden's name. "Yes," Golden responded overly sweetly.

"If you're not too busy tonight, can you come down to The V to freshen up my makeup? The job pays three hundred dollars," Tatiana said coolly.

"Sure. I don't have any plans. I just have to go home, freshen up, and check on my grandma."

"Great. See you there in about forty-five minutes. Come to the back door, Sampson will be looking for you," Tatiana said with a wink, turned on her heels, and left.

So, this was all a test to see how Golden would act under pressure? Golden was intrigued and annoyed at the same time. But she for damn sure wasn't going to let her pride get in the way of three hundred dollars. She knew The V would be packed that night, and the whole city would be out. Golden had to rush home, check on Grandma, avoid her mom, and get dressed and out the door.

Golden pulled up to The V just as the parking lot was beginning to fill. The bass from inside could be heard over the music from the cars in the parking lot. Golden tilted her rearview mirror once more to check her look. She wore a dark eyeliner that was thinly lined with a bright green highlight right above it that made her green eyes look even more intense. The rest of her makeup was simple, but flawless, topped off with a perfectly lined, deep red lip. Golden decided to wear her black body-hugging dress with a casual, oversized blue jean shirt over it. The jean shirt served a double purpose by keeping the makeup from getting all over her dress and hiding her body from peering eyes that may mistake her for the evening's entertainment.

Golden got out of her car, trying to ignore cat calls, whistles, and the "Aye shawty" she heard from the surrounding cars as weed and cheap cologne lingered in the air. She quickly made her way through the parking lot while walking on her tiptoes so her heels wouldn't sink into the gravel. Golden made it to the side entrance without anyone grabbing her. She avoided anyone trying to get her number or promising to take care of her or change her life. She knew all that would really be wanted was a night of lust with no commitment.

As she approached the door, she saw a looming figure in all black. Golden immediately felt more tense as she neared the giant-like figure.

Before Golden could get any closer, a booming voice called out to her. "Aye shawty, what you need?"

"I was told to meet Sampson at the side door," Golden stammered. "I'm here to do makeup for Tatiana."

There was a long pause while she walked up to the six-foot-four figure. He eyed her suspiciously. Then he demanded, "Lemme see your bag."

Golden opened her bag to reveal her makeup supplies. Then, without warning, the giant heavy-handedly banged on the steel door behind him with a closed fist. Golden jumped.

The door swung open, and Golden was met with loud bass booming from speakers inside the club. Her eyes were quickly met by another looming figure staring at her. His deep-set eyes scanned up and down the entirety of Golden's body. Without a word, the figure stood, staring at Golden as he sucked his gold tooth. It was Sampson, the owner of Club V. "Mmmm...mmmm...mmm...damn, you fine!"

Golden stared at Sampson, waiting for him to finish his speech, the same one he gave her every time he saw her.

"You're so fine...when you comin' ta work fa' me...you could be one of my best girls...let me take care of you...I knew your momma back in the day."

The conversation was always the same. Golden just had to endure the onslaught until Sampson got it out of his system and got back to business.

"Hey, Sampson," Golden replied dryly. "I'm here to do Tatiana's makeup." She tried to push her five-foot-ten frame past Sampson, but it didn't work. He took one step and had her cornered before she could take a step backward or slide past him.

"Tatiana...huh? So, you met her? Yeah, I sent her your way. I knew ya'll two was gonna hit it off. See how I take care of you, baby?"

Sampson showed his yellow smile again, slithering his tongue over his gold tooth.

Golden rolled her eyes and nodded.

"Well, I ain't gonna keep you from yo' money, baby, just come see ole Sampson before you leave."

Golden nodded in agreement. She already knew why Sampson wanted to see her before she left the club: he wanted his cut of the money she was going to earn doing Tatiana's makeup. Despite Sampson's love of women, his love of money was even greater. From every dollar that was made in Club V, Sampson received a cut.

CHAPTER FIVE

THAT BASS

Golden walked down the long, dark hallway leading to Club V's dressing room. With each step, she felt the bass of the speakers grow in intensity. The boom started off muffled, dull, and low, fuzzy around the edges. The closer she got to the main showroom, her stride automatically fell in step with the beat as her hips swayed in sync with the bass. Her steps grew more confident the louder the music became. The music vibrated off the walls. Her spine straightened as she lifted her head and felt the beat in her chest. She was almost to the small opening of the club floor. The bass boomed in her chest, and she could no longer feel her heartbeat. Instead, the beat of the bass consumed her. Golden looked around Club V and a smile started to spread across her lips. Beautiful women stood on pedestals, shakn' ass and titties, whatever they needed to do for the customers to part with their hard-earned dollars.

Golden loved watching the acrobatics of the dancers on the pole, but her favorite thing to watch was the women giving lap dances, whispering in men's ears, mesmerizing them with a promise of pussy. Then she heard the voice of the DJ over the bass. "Aye...we got some stallions in the house tonight. Ya'll come up outta yo' pockets and throw somethin'."

The DJ caught Golden's eye just as she passed the slight opening of the hallway to the club floor. Strobe lights, LED lights, and money being thrown was all that Golden could see. It enticed her; it seduced her.

Up ahead, Golden saw a large security guard standing in the opening of the dancers' dressing room. His body was so large that his shoulders were wider than the door and his head topped the door frame. Golden walked up to security in her long slender five-foot-ten frame. Security raised his eyebrow as he saw Golden approach. It was rare for any female to even come close to his eye level, and he was used to looking down on people. Golden walked up confidently.

"Sampson sent me. I'm here to do makeup for Tatiana."

The security guard paused for a moment because the name Tatiana did not ring a bell, but then he remembered she was the special headliner for the night. The club rarely hosted headliners, but Tatiana had met the real owner of Club V, Terrance Walker, while he was gambling in Vegas. Terrance was an ex-NFL player who had tried his hand at many businesses and failed. However, Club V was one of his most lucrative investments, primarily because it was a cash-based business. He used the money he made from Club V to support his failing ventures. Tatiana could spot a sucker from miles away and she knew how to use her beauty to get whatever she wanted. She saw Club V as a quick money trip. Tatiana had a slick business sense and was always about making money any way she could. She convinced Terrance to let her headline at Club V if she did her own promotion through social media. She told Terrance she needed a first-class, round-trip plane ticket, hotel stay, and transportation while she was in town. These were the perks of the contract she signed with Terrance. Tatiana sold

Terrance on the deal mainly because he couldn't stop staring at her titties the whole time Tatiana talked, and she made the money sound good. Terrance agreed to take fifty percent of the proceeds from the cover charge and twenty percent of what Tatiana made on stage for two nights. However, Terrance forgot to negotiate any percentage of what Tatiana made from her private dances. Tatiana also negotiated for fifty percent of what the bar earned for the two nights she was there. Terrance was a little hesitant on the terms but agreed.

Seconds after their conversation, Tatiana produced a contract from her purse that was ready for Terrance to sign. She only made it seem like Terrance negotiated a deal; he was too drunk and mesmerized by Tatiana's beauty to realized he was conned from their very first interaction. He signed the agreement without reading it or without having his lawyer preview the contract. Tatiana's signed contract stated that she would get fifty percent of the door, twenty percent of the bar, seventy percent of what she made on stage and one hundred percent of earnings from her private dances. Tatiana even had a notary on standby to make the contract legally binding before Terrance could object. She was a true businesswoman.

The security guard remembered who Tatiana was and frowned at Golden because he knew Tatiana had scammed the owner of the club. He wasn't too keen on the idea of anyone associated with Tatiana being at Club V. He looked at Golden in a disgusted manner as she impatiently shifted her bodyweight, raised her eyebrow, and pursed her lips. "So, are you gonna let me in or nawl?"

The security guard let out a deep sigh and opened the door to the dressing room. Another short, dark hallway covered in mirrors and black lighting led to the dressing room. *This is the coolest shit ever!* Golden thought. The whites of her green eyes glowed back at her as she looked in the mirrors. All that could be seen of her in the black light were her nails and the whites of her eyes glowing. She took a second to admire her own beauty and then pulled on the handle of the door to the dressing room. The room was well-lit and disarming, a stark contrast to the dimly lit hallway she'd just walked through.

As Golden's eyes adjusted, she saw half-naked women, some fully nude, doing makeup, talking in small groups, or getting dressed for the club floor. She quickly scanned the room for Tatiana before she drew too much attention. Too late.

"Hey Golden girl, what you doin' here, you dancin'?" A familiar voice called from the corner.

Golden looked; it was one of her classmates from high school, Trina, but her stage name was Buttafly. Trina had been the captain of the varsity cheerleading team. She had a lot of potential in high school but not enough drive. Trina didn't believe in herself as much as others did. Instead of taking a cheerleading scholarship to a nearby college, Trina said she was going to take a year off from school before going to college, but everyone who knew her knew she was lying. Trina was so wrapped up in her boyfriend, Troy, at the time that all she cared about was him. To keep an eye on Troy, Trina went everywhere he went and did everything he did, including smoking weed and snorting coke. Within six months of graduating high school, Trina became pregnant with her first child. Troy had convinced her to start working at Club V to make "quick money" for their family while he rode around town and sold dime bags of weed. Trina had her second child soon after the first and was now caught up in the drama and fast life of The V.

"Naw, girl. I'm here to do makeup for Tatiana," Golden replied as she craned her neck to look for Tatiana. The rest of the room fell silent as the dancers listened to Golden's and Trina's conversation while pretending not to.

"Who is Tatiana?" Trina replied in a high-pitched voice and wrinkled nose, as if Tatiana's name tasted bitter in her mouth as she said it. Trina knew exactly who Tatiana was because all the dancers, including herself, were jealous of the special attention Tatiana was getting in the club that weekend.

On cue, the door to the private dressing room opened and Tatiana floated out, naked but for a pink chiffon robe lined with feathers, giving Tatiana an angelic feel. She had on a pair of fluffy, powder-white flip-flops, and her dark hair was freshly spiral-curled, hanging neatly just below her shoulders. Tatiana had already removed the makeup Golden had applied at the mall counter just a few hours earlier. Golden walked past all the envious eyes toward the private dressing room. As she got closer to Tatiana, Golden could see how naturally beautiful she was. Tatiana walked up to Golden with her arms outstretched. "Oh, my goodness, you're finally here," Tatiana exclaimed loudly enough to make the other dancer detest her even more. She embraced Golden as she walked up to her. Golden stood frozen and confused by Tatiana's warm embrace. Their last interaction was less than friendly in Golden's memory.

Tatiana gently guided Golden through the private dressing room door and turned her head to take one last look at the envious faces in the dressing room, catching the eyes of each dancer. As she turned around, all eyes were transfixed on Tatiana's ass showing through the sheer fabric that perfectly outlined her naked body. Tatiana took one last look at the peasants and slammed the door as the sound echoed over the bassline of the music thumping in the club.

Tatiana whipped around to face Golden who was still shell-shocked from the warm greeting she had received. Golden looked around at the beautiful dressing room complete with a white, lighted, mirrored-vanity and matching plush bench. There was also a small bathroom in the suite, completed by a velvet, dark purple loveseat.

Tatiana sat at the vanity and asked Golden eagerly, "So, what did you bring?"

Golden looked at Tatiana, dumbfounded, and remained silent. She was confused by the warm welcome Tatiana was giving her. She expected their reunion to be as stale as their first encounter. Now Tatiana changed the game by embracing Golden as one of her long lost girlfriends.

"What...what is it?" Tatiana asked inquisitively.

Golden sighed and took an audible breath. She hesitantly began. "I didn't think we hit it off when we first met. Honestly, you sort of came off as a bitch. And now I walk in and you're all cool."

Tatiana smiled warmly at Golden and replied sweetly, "Aw, girl, I'm sorry. I was just in business mode. I had to make sure you were as thorough as Sampson talked you up to be."

Golden was visibly taken aback; she couldn't imagine Sampson speaking of her in a positive light. "Oh," she replied.

"Plus, when I got here, I asked some of the girls here about you and they downplayed your skills, but I looked you up online and your work is fiyah! So, I knew I had to do a pop-up and meet you."

Silence hung in the air as both women silently admired each other. Golden could smell a bullshitter from a mile away, and she knew Tatiana was being genuine when she complemented her work.

"So, why did you act so funky towards me then?" Golden asked.

"Well...people never take me seriously when they first meet me because they think that I can't be pretty and smart. So, I have to be a lil' bit of a bitch in order for them to listen to my words and not stare at my titties," Tatiana replied.

Golden understood exactly what Tatiana was saying. Golden was repeatedly overlooked because of her physical appearance. Men just wanted to obtain her, and women envied her. Women repeatedly disappointed Golden. She always wanted a tight-knit girl crew, but she never got close because women her age mostly felt insecure around her. However, Golden never thought she was better than anyone because of her looks, especially based on how she was raised by her mother. Golden constantly heard her mother say she, "wasn't shit and ain't never gonna be shit." Thank God for her grandmother who always believed in her and lifted her up. Grandmother always encouraged Golden to be the best clothing designer and makeup artist she could be.

"I can understand," Golden replied to Tatiana. "I always have people try and shade me, telling me I think I'm cute or whatever," Golden said as she hung her head.

"Don't you fucking do that!" Tatiana yelled at Golden, "Don't you ever do that!"

Golden was startled by Tatiana's sudden change in tone. Her head immediately snapped up.

"Don't you ever hang your head in shame or let another motherfucker's feelings about themselves reflect on you. People will always tell you to not do something they could never fucking do! Or they will tell you not to do something because they failed. I say fuck that and fuck them!"

Golden stood in silence for a moment, letting Tatiana's words linger in the air. No one had ever come at her that raw and honest before. Honestly, Golden couldn't think of anyone but Grandmother who gave a damn to say anything to her about her dreams. Thinking about the love and unconditional support her grandmother provided, Golden's eyes couldn't hold it together any longer and she started to tear up.

"Oh noooo!" Tatiana cooed and rushed to Golden, wiping her tears away. "Why are you crying?"

Golden silently held back her tears for a few more moments while the music played in the background. "Nobody ever gave a damn to come at me like you just did."

Tatiana put her index finger underneath Golden's chin and lift her head slowly until their eyes met. This was the first time Tatiana realized how beautiful Golden was. While fresh tears pooled in Golden's eyes, Tatiana measured her voice in a slow even tone. "Babygirl, you're the shit. Don't let nobody tell you anything different."

Tatiana ran to the bathroom and quickly grabbed some toilet paper off the roll and ran it to Golden. Golden gently wiped her eyes so as not to smear her makeup. She let out a sigh and an exacerbated laugh.

"Ugh...okay...enough of that...girl, let me beat that face and make all of these hoes jealous and take all of these men's dollas. They won't even know what hit them," Golden said while mustering a smile.

For the next hour, Golden worked on Tatiana's face, adding foundation, concealer, eye shadow, eyeliner, blush, glitter, lashes, and lipstick. Golden liked to have her clients facing away from the mirror while she worked because she didn't like for the client to be distracted and constantly looking at their progress. When Golden finally finished Tatiana's look, she slowly turned her around so she could see her reflection in the lighted vanity mirror. Tatiana's skin was smoothed to perfection, her cheekbones were accentuated, and her nose was softened but highlighted. Golden enhanced Tatiana's eyes because she remembered Grandmother telling her that the eyes were the windows to the soul. Tatiana looked at herself in disbelief; she had never seen herself look so beautiful. Her eyelashes swept her eye beautifully and the smokey eye that Golden created enhanced the color of Tatiana's light hazel eyes with hints of gold, blue, emerald green. Tatiana remembered her mentor telling her that when a man looked into a woman's eyes, he had to feel like he was the only man she'd ever had. Her mentor taught her how to seduce men and how to get more from them than they ever wanted to give.

"I love it," Tatiana told Golden. "Now let me get dressed and get into character. Go ahead and sit out front and when I come backstage you can change my makeup again for my other two looks."

Golden nodded obediently and exited the private dressing room. As she closed the door, she saw the envious faces looking back at her from the main dressing room. Golden cracked the door and said to Tatiana, "Can you please lock the dressing room door, make sure nobody steals my shit?" Then Golden strutted away with imaginary pyrotechnics going off behind her and wind blowing in her hair as she straightened her five-ten frame and stomped her way toward the main stage of The V.

CHAPTER SIX

FIRST HIT'S THA SWEETEST

Golden made her way to the main stage and passed by women dancing on laps and whispering in men's ears. Club V was super thick that night. She saw all types of men there. Men in suits, men in outdated jerseys, men with Dobbs hats and matching pantsuits. Men in jeans and fitted shirts, men in skinny jeans and designer shirts. There were white men, black men, and two small groups of Indian men.

The club's in-house DJ was yelling over the speaker as usual trying to hype the crowd. All around her she saw assess clapping, titties bouncing, and money flying. The main stage was currently occupied by Samich. Men always laughed at the name until she stepped on stage and that big, beautiful brown ass was on display. Samich had a special talent for squatting over a bottle and sandwiching it between her ass cheeks. The men went wild every time they saw her perform. Samich would get down on all fours and make her big ass bounce up and down toward the crowd, displaying her signature "earthquake" move.

Samich's ass was her most endearing quality. She had a face that most men never paid attention to because her ass was the star.

The lights in the club were synchronized to the bass of the music. Every time the bass would drop, the lights would pulsate. The club was very high-tech and advanced despite how it looked on the outside. It had the finest sound system that boomed outside the club. The two bars were always stocked with top-shelf alcohol, and the bottle girls were gorgeous and brought champagne to the tables with sparkling fanfare. Male and female attendants ensured the bathrooms were well-stocked and always clean and sanitary. The club was marketed as a high-end club in the Midwest. Although there were other strip clubs in the city and surrounding areas, Club V was known for having beautiful women and a sophisticated atmosphere. Since the club was new, it didn't have the burn holes, dingy furniture, or the smell of piss and fried food that older clubs did.

Golden found a seat at the end of the bar and ordered a bottled water. On the way to her seat, several men tried to motion her over to their table, but Golden didn't make eye contact. She'd been to Club V a few times to do some of the dancer's makeup, so she knew the ropes. She knew that if a woman was walking by herself, it was assumed that she was working. Golden didn't take offense to the assumption; she was just slightly annoyed.

The DJ played a few more songs and then the lights went down. The DJ announced that the main event was coming up. "Gentlemen! Open up your eyes and your pockets for Brilliance!"

The music started off with a deep bass thump, and then came the high-energy melody. Tatiana burst through the LED rain-curtain in an all-white, fringed, sequins-encrusted bikini top and bottoms that sparkled when the lights of the club hit it. Tatiana, aka Brilliance, prowled across the stage in her matching open-toe platform heels.

She slowly put her finger to her lips to silence the DJ. She didn't need him yelling throughout her set; she needed to seduce the men outta of their money. She didn't need someone else screaming over a microphone, disrupting her vibe. She needed to create a mood in the room. Brilliance's mentor taught her how to read and work a room while targeting the wealthiest men who came to spend hundreds. She learned the wealthiest men rarely sat near the stage, so she needed to project her essence across the room in the span of a three-minute song.

Brilliance also brought her own music for the DJ to play. She knew the type of mood she wanted to set, and she had her routine down. She knew the highs and lows of her music. She knew when to work the stage and the pole. She also knew when the music begged for her to turn up and show out. That was usually when money began to rain from the sky. If Brilliance felt the men were taking too long to get warmed up, she would focus on one man and show him so much attention that the other men would throw money just to be a part of that man's fantasy. Brilliance never made personal contact with the client: she knew that was reserved for the private dance room where the real money was made. The main floor was just the appetizer. She kept the first session short, just to warm up the crowd and build the anticipation for her second performance.

Her first performance sold the fantasy of the good girl: the angel fantasy. Her second performance focused on her being the nasty stripper, showcasing her death-drop pole tricks, splits, and floor work. Her mentor taught her that floor work would draw the men in closer to see her, and then they would make it rain all over her naked body. Her final performance featured all her pole work tricks where she hung from the ceiling and twirled on the pole as if gravity were only a mindset. Afterward, Brilliance exited the stage and immediately headed to the dressing room. Her quick set caught Golden off guard and must've caught Sampson off guard too because he quickly moved backstage to confront Brilliance. Golden quickly capped her bottled water and made her way back to the dressing room because she didn't want to miss the showdown that was about to ensue between Tatiana and Sampson.

When Golden returned to the private dressing room, she heard Sampson yelling over the music. "What in the fuck was that? So, you just think 'cuz you sucked a nigga's dick then you can come in here and do what you want?"

"Actually, no, I don't think anything," Tatiana replied coolly. "I know what I can do per the contract I have signed with the owner of the club, who consequently is not you. And per said contract, if I'm not allowed to perform according to the parameters of my contract with the owner of the club, not you, then my contract is in breech and therefore I am due $500,000. I will get said $500,000 if my contract is not carried out to the T. Now, if you would like to make decisions for your boss and the owner of this club, then I can leave and have my lawyer contact you. If not, then I need you to please close my dressing room door so that I can get ready for my private dances."

Sampson stood there fuming and turning Tatiana's words over in his head. All he could hear was *$500,000*. He knew he couldn't go over Terrance's head, no matter how much he wanted to throw Tatiana out on her smart-ass. Sampson's face grew redder and redder by the second as he silently fumed over Tatiana's words. He was the one all the dancers, bartenders, security guards, and bottle girls feared, but he was not the one who truly had decision-making power at Club V; Tatiana and Sampson both knew that. She humiliated Sampson in front of his whole staff, and he had to regain control of the club quickly before everyone started to question his authority and revolt.

Sampson glared at Tatiana and turned on his heels. He hissed, "Bitch" under his breath and walked away. "You bitches stop gawking and get to fucking work. Ain't nobody paying ya'll to sit around and look at me!" Sampson banged the dressing room door with his open palm, and it sounded over the bass of the music. The dressing room was quiet and still while the dancers tried to process the scene that had taken place.

After a few moments, the whole dressing room started to come back to life with a low buzz. Tatiana had just super-flexed on Sampson in a way they only imagined having the courage to do. The energy instantly changed, and the girls had a new respect for Tatiana. Golden cleared her throat. "So, do you want to get started on your next look?"

"Absolutely," Tatiana replied. She turned on her heels and entered the private dressing room.

"Biiiiiitch...OMG...that was everything, girl! The way you served his ass, that's what he gets. I've never heard a stripper talk like you before," Golden exclaimed as soon as she closed the private dressing room door.

Tatiana whipped her head around with a frown. "That's because I'm not a stripper or a dancer, I'm a businesswoman."

Silence filled the air, and Golden stood awkwardly. She measured her next words carefully, but Tatiana broke the silence.

"Look, I'm sorry. I didn't mean to snap. It just pisses me off when women are always looked down upon, especially when you're pretty. It's like all they expect for us to do is to sit and look pretty. And I make them pay for it because they never see me coming."

There was another awkward silence, and Golden started rustling uneasily through her makeup bag. She started to set up the second look they discussed earlier. Golden began to remove the previous look with her favorite makeup wipes. She was grateful that Tatiana let her work in silence because it gave Golden an opportunity to think about Tatiana's words. She, too, felt resentful of people who never expected anything more from her than being pretty. Golden oftentimes felt like no one really saw her. She felt like no one would ever take her seriously as a fashion designer because she looked more like a model.

As she worked, Golden wished she had more confidence like Tatiana. She wondered where that strength came from. She wished she had the type of fierceness and surety that made Tatiana unafraid to speak to Sampson like she did. Golden also wondered where Tatiana learned how to write up a contract. She'd never heard of a stripper having a contract before, and for $500,000! *Whoa...that was some serious cash,* Golden thought. She spent the rest of the time finishing Tatiana's second look while fantasizing about what she would do with $500,000.

Golden looked on as Brilliance took the stage. She mesmerized the crowd with the sway of her hips and the bounce of her perfectly-placed titties. Her small waist and pear-shaped ass in customized black leather with deep purple sequins were unforgettable. Golden completed Brilliance's look with a heavy smoky eye with purple highlight in the waterline, completed by purple jewels on Brillance's upper eyelid. Brilliance spent a few moments on the main stage, then she worked her way through the crowd. Toward the end of her set, she stopped at a table in the back and did a very slow dance, whispering in the customer's ear. She then grabbed his hand and led him to the private dance area.

Golden didn't see Tatiana reemerge for a while, so she figured Brilliance was still in the private room. Golden passed the time by watching the main stage room. She was amazed at all the money flying around. She envisioned herself dancing on stage and men throwing money at her. She imagined the different looks she would create with hair, makeup, and costumes. She could create a whole persona and really get paid. In all the times she visited the club, she never envisioned herself being a stripper because she looked down on them. She could never understand how a woman could take off her clothes for money and spread her legs for every man in the building to see. Although, after watching Tatiana all night, her point of view changed. She now saw that these women had the power. Men came in night after night willing to spend their money on them, just to see their bodies bend and sway to the bass and lights of the club. Golden was seduced by the mental image of her swirling and grinding to the music while rubbing dollars all over her naked breast.

"Hell yeah...get that shit," a man nearby whispered.

Golden didn't realize she had closed her eyes and was swaying to the beat, slowly grinding to the music in her chair. She abruptly stopped and opened her eyes, embarrassed. She had lost all sense of time and space. She quickly scurried away from the table and headed back to the dressing room. She hurried past two girls in the dressing room hallway, while one of the girls intentionally bumped into Golden.

"Watch out, damn!" The other dancer replied. Both of the girls walked quickly onto the dance floor, but Golden barely noticed their behavior because she was still embarrassed about how caught up in the lights and music she had been.

Golden barged into the private dressing room. She was relieved to not see Tatiana. Golden collapsed in the chair in front of the lighted vanity in a disheveled heap. She slowly raised her head and looked at herself—really looked at herself. She raised her chin and admired the length of her neck. She slowly turned her head from side to side, appreciating her own beauty. Then her gaze shifted to her green eyes. As she peered into them, her eyes stared back and then began to fill with tears.

Golden shook her head and looked away in shame. She didn't know why she was crying. Was it because she was disappointed in herself for not applying to fashion school? Or was she upset because all she heard was her mother's voice telling her she wasn't gonna be shit? Or was it because she was ashamed that she could never live up to the expectations of her grandmother? Was it due to her feeling desirable only in a strip club? Or was it... just everything? Golden covered her eyes with her hands and tried to gather herself as the tears began to fall, despite her trying to hold them back.

Just then, Tatiana walked into the dressing room. "Hey girl, I was wondering where you were, I just made three stacks off that..." her voice trailed off when she noticed Golden wiping away tears. "What's wrong?" Tatiana rushed over to Golden and knelt next to her. "Tell me."

"It's nothing...just everything," Golden sniffed. "I just wanna be more, like...like what you said. I wanna be more than just pretty."

Tatiana looked Golden deep in her eyes and softly replied, "I know."

Golden excused herself and went to the small bathroom to collect herself so she could finish Tatiana's final look for the night. Tatiana asked Golden to stay after she completed tip-out so she could pay her.

Brilliance's second set went even better than the first. This time, Golden stayed in the private dressing room and lay down on the plush, purple couch. She was emotionally drained from the day and needed a moment to herself. Golden quickly fell asleep despite all the commotion in the dressing room and the loud booming music of the main stage. She was startled awake by Tatiana opening the dressing room door and dumping a duffel bag full of cash on the floor with a loud thud.

"Oh, my bad. Did I wake you? I didn't notice you were over there," Tatiana said as she plopped down beside Golden. Tatiana smelled like a mixture of alcohol, various colognes, weed, and cigarettes. She unzipped her thigh-high boots and struggled to get them off. Golden stood to offer assistance, gave a hard tug, and scooted Tatiana halfway off the couch. Both girls fell over in laughter. "Dang girl, you gonna pull my whole foot off," Tatiana said as she scooted back on the couch between laughs. Golden sat back on the couch.

Tatiana dragged her duffel bag over to her side. Then she got up and rifled through the bags she brought and turned around, producing a money counter. Golden's eyes grew wide with wonder. She'd only seen the dope boys in her neighborhood and people in music videos use a money counter. Tatiana cleared the small, glass coffee table and began separating her bills by denomination to get them ready to count. Golden watched in awe. She had never seen a stripper with this much cash before! Tatiana didn't hide anything from Golden. She reached into her bookbag and pulled out a laptop. She began logging her income from the night. Golden sat in awe of Tatiana; she really was a businesswoman.

After Tatiana accounted for all her money made that night, she calculated how much she owed Club V and set that aside. Then, she handed over a stack of money to Golden. "It's $2,500 for the night."

Golden reluctantly took the stack of money. It was well over the amount of money she made each month as a manager and doing makeup on the side. "Thank you so much! I don't know what to say."

"You deserve it, Golden, and so much more," Tatiana replied. "Do you know why I asked you to stay for the whole night? I wanted to see how you moved. You weren't easily swayed by any of these whack-ass bitches in here or these thirsty-ass niggas. You just need to get your confidence up, lil' Momma."

They smiled at each other. Golden didn't even think Tatiana had noticed her or even cared enough to compliment her.

"I think you have a real talent for makeup. You should put it to use," Tatiana said with a reassuring nod.

"Well...honestly, tonight made me think about dancing. You think I can do it?" Golden eagerly waited for Tatiana's response.

"You could be one of the baddest bitches in the game if you keep your head on straight. I can teach you how to do that, how to move out here. But you gotta get confidence on your own."

Golden nodded in agreement, putting her money in her bag. She got up and started to put away her brushes and pack her makeup.

"I'm here the whole weekend. Come over to my hotel room and I'll give you a crash course. Show you how to spot a man with money. I say man and not nigga, 'cuz a nigga ain't gonna spend no real money. But a man will spend real money with you and only you. He knows what he wants when he comes through the door. I can teach you how to sell him that fantasy. Teach you how to talk to him and how to keep these snake-ass bitches off you. Deal?"

"Bet!" Golden replied.

Just then, Sampson busted through the door. "Time to cash out." He stood with his hands on his hips, trying to restore his menacing demeanor he had lost earlier. Tatiana sighed, grabbed two stacks of cash she already set aside, and handed them to Sampson.

He looked around the room and noticed the money counter and laptop, and he thought it wise not to question the amount of cash she was handing him.

"Same place, same time tomorrow?" Tatiana questioned.

"Humph," Sampson said and walked away. "Aye! Time to cash out! Run me ya'll's money!" Sampson yelled at the other dancers. Tatiana walked to the dressing room door and closed it.

"I'll text you the info for my hotel room. You good getting home?"

"Yeah, I'll have one of the bouncers walk me to my car," Golden replied.

"Oh, and can you do my makeup tomorrow and Sunday, too? $2500 a night?" Tatiana said coolly.

"Cool. See you tomorrow." Just then, Golden's phone chimed. She looked at the incoming text.

You good? Ain't see your car yet.

The text was from Marquez.

"Booty call? Okay, Ms. Golden!" Tatiana teased.

Golden shrugged off Tatiana's teasing. She didn't want to admit that's exactly what she had been using Marquez as for the past year. She had to admit: sex with him felt right. He knew how to hold her tight and whisper in her ear how beautiful she was while he was deep inside her.

Had a gig…on my way home, Golden quickly texted back.

"Anyway, girl. I'll see you tomorrow. And thank you for this," Golden said as she patted her bag where she stashed her money. "Thanks for everything," she said even quieter.

Chapter Seven

Romeo Without Juliet

G olden texted Marquez.

It was nearly three am and Marquez was feigning to see Golden again. Of course, he was awake, waiting for her text. He couldn't get their last encounter out of his mind. Golden had been his fantasy woman since ninth grade. She was fine, book and street-smart, sweet with some sass, and knew how to put it down in the bedroom. Marquez saw Golden's potential. He knew all about the stress her mother put her through growing up because he had a front-row seat. Marquez grew up across the street from Golden. He watched and waited for her to turn into a woman before he made his move. Plus, he wasn't even sure Golden would be interested in him. He always thought Golden looked at him as a friend, but he hoped for much more.

One night after a long talk about their exes, Golden and Marquez got a little carried away. He didn't know if it was the brown liquor or the new strain of weed he had copped earlier, but the next thing he knew, Golden was straddling over him in his parked car in front of his momma's house, tonguing him down. He didn't hesitate or stop to ask if she was sure because she was clearly intoxicated. That was the one time he regretted sleeping with a woman. He wanted the first time to be special between Golden and him, instead of rushed and in the heat of the moment. Marquez couldn't believe he was finally sleeping with the woman he fantasized about night after night, stroking himself to sleep in high school. Of course, he busted quick, but he assured himself that he gave Golden the best twelve pumps of her life. They had a few other encounters, but he insisted they go to a hotel from then on so he could really show her all that she'd been missing over the years. Their meet-up spot was a hotel by the highway at the edge of town. He would get the room and then text her the room number. He always had alcohol, weed, and candles or some other trinket to help set the mood.

Marquez texted Golden the address as usual and she went up to the room. He opened the door with a big smile; he was always happy to see her. Golden gave him a half-smile. She was totally mentally exhausted from her evening at The V. Her head was still swirling from Tatiana's words. She was left feeling even more inadequate and self-conscious about her life decisions than before. How could a stranger have more confidence in her skills than she did? Why had she not used her sex as a weapon and made men pay for her time like her mother? Why couldn't she be a hustler like Mother Rose? Why...why...why?

"Hey, babe, you good?" Marquez's voice snapped Golden out of her internal monologue.

Golden needed to be touched and worshipped. She wanted to feel that ecstasy that silenced her brain. Golden simply nodded and pushed Marquez toward the bed. She could already feel him stiffen in his jeans. That's what she liked about him; he was always ready to please her. Golden straddled Marquez and kissed him deeply, more deeply than she ever had. She needed him to feel her urgency. She needed him to feel how much she craved the closeness of his body. Marquez followed suit and returned an even deeper kiss and breathed in Golden's air as he slowly rolled his tongue on hers. They began to feverishly undress each other, clothes flying everywhere. Marquez flipped Golden over in one simple movement and was quickly hovering over her. He paused for a moment and stared into Golden's eyes. He saw so much fire and wanting in her eyes that he dove in again and kissed her deeply.

"You are so beautiful, Golden Rose," Marquez whispered softly as he kissed Golden's neck. He was one of the few people that insisted on calling her by her full name. He moved down to her breast and devoured Golden while she grew more aroused with each flick of his tongue. Their passion ended with Golden reaching her peak twice before Marquez finally gave in to the feeling of erotic pleasure and collapsing in a soft, satisfied mound on top of Golden.

She loved to feel him climax because he worked so hard to please her. Marquez was truly an unselfish lover. He slowly pulled out of Golden, carefully holding onto the condom, always making sure to keep Golden safe. She admired that about him. Golden could always let go, knowing that Marquez would always do the right thing and protect her; he always had, even when they were kids. Marquez got up and went to the bathroom to clean up while Golden lay there in bliss and drifted off to sleep. She was fast asleep when Marquez came out of the bathroom. He simply put on some shorts and sat in a chair across the room and watched Golden sleep. He admired how beautiful she was even in her sleep. He thought to himself that he could wake up to this beautiful creature every morning if she would let him. He noticed Golden wince and slightly shudder. He pulled the heavy hotel sheet over her and took a soft blanket from his overnight bag and placed it over Golden's naked body. He noticed her body relax as she sighed and drifted into an even deeper sleep.

The next morning Golden awoke to waffles, bacon, and coffee from her favorite places. Marquez was across the room working on his laptop and finishing up his breakfast. Marquez didn't notice that Golden was awake yet. So, she took the opportunity to admire Marquez's body and how fine he was. He stood six three with a short cut with 360 waves. He had tattoos of some of the artwork his deceased brother created on his back, chest, and arms. She could see his fit physique peeking from underneath his close-fitting shirt. She stopped lusting as she got to Marquez's fingernails. Since he worked as an auto mechanic, he sometimes still had dirt and grease under his nails. She rolled her eyes and cleared her throat. "Hey, you...good morning," she said with a forced smile.

Marquez didn't hear her because he had his earbuds in. He was always listening to some podcast or online training. He would try to get Golden to listen, but her patience was very thin for things that did not readily interest her. Marquez was super focused on whatever was on his laptop screen, so Golden decided to wrap up in her sheet and begin to enjoy her breakfast.

Marquez noticed Golden out of the corner of his eye. He removed his ear buds and closed his laptop. "Good morning, Golden Rose," Marquez's voice hummed. "How did you sleep?" he asked with a smirk. He knew that she slept well.

"I slept good," Golden replied with a half-smile and began unwrapping her food.

"You got kinda freaky last night, huh?" Marquez asked.

Golden hated when he stated the obvious. It was one of the things that kept her detached from him and prevented her from further developing feelings for Marquez.

Golden kept eating her food and ignored Marquez's question. "Yeah, I had a rough night," she eventually replied after finishing her entire meal. She never once looked in his direction, but she could feel his eyes on her the entire time she ate. *Why is he just staring at me like that*? Golden thought. She became even more irritated because Marquez didn't say anything to her, nor did he interrupt her breakfast or rush her into answering his question. His patience was unnerving.

While Golden was too busy being irritated by his presence, Marquez just sat, admiring her beauty and enjoying being in Golden Rose's presence. He loved her for as long as he could remember, and he never thought there would ever be a time when he wouldn't. He knew Golden was materialistic, but he also understood that was because of her upbringing. He saw the men coming and going for her mother. He noticed the kinds of cars they drove and the jewelry they flashed to entice Althea. Apparently it worked. He would hear a car door close in the middle of the night and Althea's erratic footsteps dragging on the concrete sidewalk leading up to her front porch. He could hear Althea curse to herself while drunk, looking for her house key. Sometimes, Golden would hear her and answer the door, but he noticed as she got older, Golden no longer waited for her mother to come home at night. Marquez wanted to be a stable light in Golden's life; that's why he never pressed or pressured her about anything. In his eyes, she could do no wrong. He simply wanted to provide a life for Golden so she could concentrate on her goals and dreams for once. That is why he worked so hard at the garage. He saved and spent his money wisely, but his biggest accomplishment was investing in the stock market.

Marquez was always smart and curious. Whenever he didn't know an answer to something, his mother advised him to look it up. This simple practice of doing his own research paid off, and Marquez had made quite a nest egg for himself through investing. However, he never told anyone of his endeavors because he feared the scrutiny he would come under from his friends and Golden. He didn't want anyone to think that he was above them or better than them. He only wanted to create a better life for his mother and himself. He wanted to give Golden the life she so deserved.

Marquez crossed the room toward Golden and bent down from behind to give her a hug. He inhaled her scent with a deep breath and enjoyed just holding her. He knew she wouldn't allow him to embrace her for long. On cue, Golden slightly shrugged Marquez off and stood up to face him. "Thank you for breakfast and last night," Golden said sweetly. She slowly gathered herself and went to the bathroom to shower.

Marquez moved his attention back to his laptop. *If only Golden could love me like I love her,* Marquez thought. His dream was to marry Golden at a destination wedding and then move to the Southwest and enjoy the beautiful backdrop of the desert. How could he make her understand the depth of his love and affection for her? All he wanted to do was love her and take away the pain of not having her father and living with a dysfunctional mother. If only she would let him in.

As Golden showered, she recounted the events of the previous night. She thought about how much of a boss Tatiana was. She thought about how much she wanted to be just like her. And the money she made the night before was super dope, and she was ready to make more. She couldn't wait to go back to Club V that night!

She thought about all the money Tatiana counted and how much she would count tonight. Could she make that much money stripping? She was curious and wanted Tatiana to teach her how.

Chapter Eight

LIFESTYLES OF THE HOOD RICH

Golden had been working at Pinky's Kitten for about seven months. Tatiana taught Golden to never strip in the same city she lived in because seeing her customers at the local Walmart would never be a pleasant, chance meeting. She bought herself a used BMW, all-white with peanut butter interior. She wanted a newer model, but Tatiana told her to only buy what she could afford without having a car payment. So, she talked to Marquez about what type of car she could buy.

Of course, Marquez accompanied Golden to the car dealership to buy a certified pre-owned BMW. Marquez told her he could perform any additional engine work she needed. He checked the car once she made her final decision, and he was even able to negotiate a lower sticker price for her because he knew a lot more about cars than she did. Marquez also impressed Golden with his knowledge of interest rates and buying a car in general. Marquez was shocked when Golden brought out a stack of cash to pay for her vehicle. However, that particular car dealership required a certified cashier's check to complete the transaction.

"So, what do you mean, my money isn't good enough?" Golden questioned the finance personnel at the car dealership.

"No ma'am, it's not that, I assure you," the finance person replied. "It's just that we have certain requirements on our end to ensure proper bookkeeping."

"I can just call my personal banker and have him cut a cashier's check and then you can give me the cash," Marquez said nonchalantly. "My bank is only a few blocks away, and I can make it happen right now if you really want me to."

"Okay...sure," Golden replied hesitantly. Where in the heck did Marquez get all that money from and when? Golden had so many questions swirling around in her head, but she couldn't focus on that right then because she needed a reliable vehicle to get back and forth to Pinky's Kitten.

Most of the time she caught rides from girls who lived in her hometown or who worked at both Club V and Pinky's Kitten. But she was growing tired of waiting on girls to finish with their last customers and engaging in small talk during the forty-five-minute ride home.

Golden saved her money just how Tatiana taught her. She also followed Tatiana's guidance on how to make more money than any other girl in the club. Golden was a committed student of Tatiana's and felt so grateful that their paths crossed.

Tatiana was now Golden's mentor and friend. Golden soaked up all the information Tatiana gave her. Golden knew Tatiana wasn't giving her "free game," she knew that Tatiana's mentoring would come at a price. What that price was, Golden didn't know just yet. But in the meantime, she decided to enjoy the ride!

Golden worked at Pinky's Kitten for about six months before getting caught up in the night life of the club. She began to drink with the customers and bartenders. Golden even began smoking weed here and there, depending on how much money her customer at the time was throwing. Golden, ignoring Tatiana's advice to not get caught up in the drinking and drugs of the club's nightlife, thought she could handle it. She continued working at Pinky's Kitten while attempting to maintain her assistant managers position at the mall's makeup counter. Golden didn't notice, but her appearance at her day job began to wane. She cared less and less about her appearance at the mall because most of the time she was operating on a few hours of sleep or a hard night of partying.

Golden's sales also began to slip because she was a no-call-no-show for many of her shifts. Her manager saw Golden careening toward an end that she knew all too well. "Hey Golden, can I talk to you for a moment in the back?" asked Angela, the head of the beauty department.

"Yeah," Golden replied in a dry, irritated voice. She was not in the mood for one of Angela's pep talks about numbers and making the customer happy. Angela was always concerned with the bottom line and how much their department sold, and she didn't like to hear excuses, just results. Golden already had her excuse prepared as to why her sales slipped in the past few weeks. *Heck, I'm the number one earner here anyway, she betta not say anything to me,* Golden thought.

"Golden, come with me to the back," Angela motioned her hand in a sweeping gesture to the breakroom.

Golden huffed and stormed off to the backroom without an answer. *I really don't have time for this bullshit. I came in here today as a damn kindness to them. My feet hurt and I am still halfway drunk from last night,* Golden rambled in her head.

"Golden, are you alright?" Angela spoke so softly that Golden barely heard her through the tantrum Golden was throwing in her own head. Angela leaned in further to try to catch Golden's eye. "Sweetie, are you alright?"

When Golden finally heard Angela and registered her voice, she jerked her head back, enraged. "What do you mean, 'am I alright?'" Golden had a major attitude and was irritated because she was sleep-deprived and still had alcohol in her system.

"Look...Golden, I like you and I'm here to help," Angela said in a concerned tone. Golden didn't reply so Angela continued. "You've been one of our top sellers, if not our top seller in the whole makeup department, since you started working here. I don't know if you're going through problems at home with your mother or what?" Angela leaned back to measure Golden's demeanor. She knew that Golden's mother was an alcoholic and Golden was really the only one working in her household. She also knew that Golden took care of her grandmother as well. Angela thought that a raise would help take some of the pressure off Golden. She thought Golden would be relieved and appreciative. "I sense that you may be going through some things at home, so I want to offer you a two-dollar-an-hour raise."

Angela leaned in even further and spoke in a gentler manner. "I knew your mother in high school. And I knew she had a hard time after your father got killed." Angela paused to check Golden's response, then decided to proceed. "My husband works for the police department, and you know, people talk. I know your mother has been picked up a few times for prostitution." Angela's voice trailed off because Golden looked up with a fire in her eyes that she'd never seen before. "I...I...I mean, I thought, I mean I know that you may be having money issues and you've been missing shifts, so I thought a raise would help," Angela said.

Golden stood up slowly and moved toward Angela, her heart beating through her ears. *The audacity of this bitch!* Golden thought. *What, does she think I am out here selling pussy like my momma, and who the fuck is she to judge me or my momma?*

Golden moved closer and spoke very slowly with as much venom as she could muster. "Bitch, you need to be worried about your husband at the strip club and spending all ya'll money at Club V. You the one that needs a raise, funky bitch! Ask yo' husband how much money he spends at Club V when you think he's pulling security. He stay buying pussy in that motherfucker! You need to worry about your own house! And as far as me and my momma go, bitch, don't you ever speak on my family again unless you prepared to die." Golden continued to stare at Angela to make sure she knew that Golden was dead serious.

"Fuck you and this job! I quit!" Golden snatched off her smock and threw it at Angela's chest and walked out of the back office. With each step Golden took she began to feel the release of hot tears on her face. Who did Angela think she was and why did she think it was okay to talk about her mother? *My momma don't have anything to do with this damn job,* Golden fumed.

As Golden made her way to her car, she sat there for a while and thought about the confrontation she just had with Angela. She couldn't believe that Angela came at her like that, mentioning her mother and then adding insult to injury by giving her a two-dollar raise that she should've gotten months ago.

Moments later, Golden thought about her time spent at the makeup counter and how much she would miss seeing her customers and making them feel beautiful. Now she had to focus on her new hustle: dancing and finessing these men out of their paychecks. Golden put on her sunglasses, sat up straight, checked her reflection in her rearview mirror, and pulled away.

Chapter Nine

RECKLESS DEVOTION

Golden stormed through the door and jolted her mother awake on the couch. "What the hell wrong wit chu?" Althea was still groggy from the night before and hated being awakened until she was fully ready. She repeated, "What's wrong wit chu?"

"I'm not in the mood, Momma, I just quit my job!" Golden was still irritated from the confrontation she had with Angela, and the last thing she needed was to have to explain to her mother why she'd just quit.

"So, what you gonna do now?" Althea asked while wiping the sleep out of her eyes. "I can take care of me, but I can't take care of me, you, and Grandma."

"You never have," Golden spat out the words before she could even stop herself.

"Oh...so you all high and mighty, huh? You ain't too big to get yo' ass whooped, little girl!" Althea was always ready for a fight with

Golden. She couldn't stand how Golden paraded around the house like she was God's gift to the world.

"Look, Momma, I'm not trying to argue and fight with you. I just lost my job and now I gotta get on my hustle, period. I'll just work more weekends at the club now," Golden resigned quietly.

"Oh, so now you gonna be a full-time ass shaker huh? You like showing all them men yo' pussy, huh?" Althea was full of hate today.

"At least I get paid for showing my pussy and not fucking for free like you!" Golden screamed at the top of her lungs. She was tired and frustrated. Golden was sick of being a caretaker and never receiving not one thank you from her mother.

"Oh, so you think you the shit now, huh? You think 'cuz these men out here throwing these dollas that you the shit? You think you better than me?" Althea began to stand and adjust her robe. Her eyes became fiercely fixed on Golden's face. "You think because you show yo' pussy in a club you better than me? Well, baby girl, lemme tell you something, we both hoes, I'm just honest about my shit! I learned a long time ago that these so-called men don't care nothing about you when they leave that club. You ain't the shit to them, you just another hoe!" Althea was now walking toward Golden aggressively.

Golden backed up because she knew the telltale signs of when her mother was about go into a fit of rage, and she never knew where that rage would take her. One time, Althea lost control when Golden was thirteen years old and pushed her hard onto the floor. Golden hit her head and had to get three stitches to close the wound. Her grandma took Golden to the hospital on the city bus to get the stitches. While they were on the bus, Grandma prepped Golden on what to say about how she received her head injury. She told Golden that she could get taken away from her mother and sent to live in a foster home and her mother would go to jail. So, Golden lied and told the ER staff that she fell off her bike and hit her head even though she didn't even own a bicycle. Golden remembered having a throbbing headache for days afterward. After that day, Golden never got too close to Althea when she was worked up.

Golden quickly walked away and went to her room. "Where yo' punk ass going?" Althea yelled after her.

Golden didn't respond. She quickly retrieving the cash she'd been stashing from working at Pinky's Kitten from various hiding spaces in her room. She didn't trust her mother. By the time she reached her second to last hiding spot Althea was standing in the doorway fuming. "Where you think you going? You little bitch! You think you can..." Althea's voice trailed off once she saw the stacks of money Golden was stuffing into bookbags.

Golden felt Althea's stares but continued to quickly pack her things. She knew that she could no longer live in the house with her mother. She had to go right then. Golden didn't want a physical confrontation with her mother, but she knew that her mother's jealousy of Golden's money would quickly turn into rage.

"Oh, I see, you been holding out on me. You been stackn' yo' little chips I see. I found one of yo' stashes so I didn't think you was poppn' yo' pussy like that. Now I see you been holding out on me?" Althea was now calm. Golden, quickly taking her eyes away from her task, looked at Althea to measure her frame of mind, but she never stopped her hands from moving and packing.

Golden knew that Althea found her stash a long time ago. Once Althea found out that Golden was working at Pinky's Kitten, she began to search her room for cash regularly, but she only looked in a few places. Golden kept track of the money Althea stole and would use those hiding spots as an allowance for Althea. Golden figured the more her mother stole from her, the less she had to deal with those nasty men she soiled herself with in return for a utility bill, drugs, or alcohol. However, Golden would never further humiliate her mother by letting Althea know that she knew she was stealing. Golden knew that Althea's fragile ego would never accept help from her own daughter, so she let her think she was stealing. Golden finished packing a few items and decided she would come for the rest of her things when Althea was out for the evening or passed out on the couch. Golden was relieved that Grandmother was at dialysis and didn't have to see her leave. She decided she would come by the house the next day and talk to Grandmother about her decision to move out.

As Golden finished packing, she grabbed a small stack of money and walked up to Althea. "Here." Golden stood there holding the cash and avoiding eye contact with Althea. Althea's pride did not get the best of her this time, and she took the money as Golden pushed past her. "I just need to get away for a minute and clear my head, Momma," Golden lied. She wanted to put as much distance and space between her mom and all the dysfunction of her past. She wanted to be free.

"So, you not gonna take any of your sketch pads?" Althea's voice softened as she spoke to Golden's back. Golden stopped dead in her tracks. She never thought her mother noticed any of her drawings. Grandmother was the only one who'd ever seen Golden's sketches and one of the few people who encouraged her to apply to fashion school. Golden never thought for a moment that Althea even knew about Golden's passion for fashion and creating head-to-toe looks. Without turning her head Golden replied, "I'll be back for 'em, Momma." Then she walked out the front door and closed it softly.

A wave of emotion hit Golden as she walked to the car with so many unanswered questions. *Did her mother really love her? When did her mother notice her sketches?* Golden's head was swirling. As she got inside her car, she threw her bags in the passenger seat. The tears started to stream down her face for the second time that day, but this time these were tears of sadness instead of anger. *I thought she never even noticed me,* Golden thought. Just then, Golden's eyes shot to the front window of the house as she saw Althea looking after her through the sheer curtains. Her mother never appeared so fragile until that moment. She didn't see her as an adversary, just as a broken woman. They locked eyes and held each other's gaze. Then, Golden put her car in reverse and slowly backed out of her driveway. Golden sobbed even harder because she could still see Althea looking out the window after her. And for a moment Golden thought, *Now whose gonna take care of her?*

CHAPTER TEN

MISGUIDED RAGE

When Althea was growing up, she was always praised for her light skin and hazel eyes. She was what was considered as "in" during the early 90s. Althea grew up in a middle-class, black community that was long cut off from convenience stores and gas stations. Her community was riddled with liquor stores and corner boys. Althea knew Mother Rose didn't have a typical nine-to-five, but she didn't care because she was always the best dressed in the hood. Mother Rose was a born hustler, and her currency was street cred. Everyone in the hood knew Mother Rose; she was the best booster in the city, especially for clothes and shoes. She boosted from malls and stores spanning from the Midwest to the East Coast.

When Althea was growing up, she had all the latest 90s fashions from up-and-coming hip-hop brands and major fashion house brands; she loved to mix and match styles. Mother Rose was "hood rich" and didn't care about anything other than looking good and smearing it in the faces of neighbors. Mother Rose always told Althea, "Now go to school and show out! They ain't ready for my baby girl."

And Althea ate up every word! She always walked through the halls of her high school with her head held high, sporting an imaginary crown. Her mindset was centered around her physical beauty, clothes, and shoes. Most of the girls in school thought Althea was stuck up and underserving of the attention she garnered from the boys, but Althea thought high school boys were beneath her because they couldn't do anything for her.

Attention was Althea's drug of choice, be it good or bad. It got her high seeing people envy her, whispering behind her back with jealously. She devilishly relished at the envious look in her high school teacher's eyes when she strolled into class with a $500 handbag, and she was only a sophomore. But everyone knew Mother Rose's occupation and how Althea got her wares. She mistakenly interpreted people's looks of pity for envy. Some of the teachers were Mother Rose's old classmates and they could see Althea headed down the same dead-end path as her mother.

Althea didn't make friends easily because she was always in competition with other girls, save one: her best friend, Shaunice. Shaunice and Althea grew up in the same neighborhood and their mothers were childhood friends. So, naturally, the two girls became friends as well. Shaunice was as sweet and accommodating as Althea was aggressive and narcissistic, but the friendship between the two worked, if, and only if, Shaunice continued playing her subservient role.

One day at lunchtime, Althea noticed Shaunice talking to the most popular boy in eleventh grade, Michael Kinney, in the courtyard. Judging from Michael's body language and wide smile, he was really into Shaunice. Althea stood from afar, drinking her soda, her throat tightening with jealousy. She noticed how Shaunice sheepishly looked into Michael's eyes, returning his smile while a nervous half-grin played on her lips.

Althea looked on as the beginning of a love story played out right before her eyes. She knew that her best friend Shaunice had had a crush on Michael Kinney since the year before. All Shaunice did was daydream about being with Michael. For the last two months, Shaunice had talked about Michael every day on their ride home from school. Althea knew how much Shaunice liked Michael, and for an instant a small smile played on Althea's lips because she was happy for her friend. She happily stared at the couple, but then a flip switched. Althea began to look at Shaunice's appearance and pick her apart.

She thought, *What does he even see in her anyway?* Althea began to critique her best friend's looks. Shaunice had on some faded jeans with an oversized, lavender sweater that was a hand-me-down from Shaunice's older sister. She had on some patent leather shoes with lace bows that Althea decided were cute because Mother Rose copped a matching pair for Althea and her. Althea physically shook her head to shake away those images and feelings of friendship. In this moment, Althea was trying to dissect Shaunice to figure out exactly what was making Michael smile so hard and gaze so intently at her friend. Then Althea looked up at Shaunice's hair. It was all over her head as usual. Shaunice had hair past her shoulders, but she always wore her hair in a ponytail with frayed edges sticking out at the sides. Althea then decided, *She's not prettier than me.* She finished her soda, sauntering across the courtyard toward the budding couple.

"Hey ya'll...what ya'll over here talking about?" Althea called out loudly, knowing the sudden attention would embarrass her friend. She darted a mischievous look back and forth between Shaunice and Michael.

"Oh, hey Thea," Shaunice stammered. "We were just chilln'." Then Shaunice, snuck a look at Michael's smooth chocolate brown skin while he was focused on Althea.

Damn, he is fine, Althea thought.

Michael gave Althea a nod then turned his focus back onto Shaunice. Althea became a little irritated because she was used to stealing boys' attention away from any girl they were crushing on. Shaunice noticed Althea's slight irritation and wanted to escape from the uncomfortable situation.

"Hmmm...ya'll look mighty cozy to me," Althea asserted.

"Ummm" Shaunice shifted from her left foot to her right, nervously. "Mike and I were just talking about tonight's basketball game. He asked if we were going."

Michael shot Shaunice a questioning look. He was surprised about what was coming out of Shaunice's mouth because he had just professed how much he liked her and how he had been eying her from quite some time. He told her how much he liked that she wasn't pressed for any boy's attention, unlike her boy-crazy friend. And he was attracted to how smart she was. He also acknowledged how focused she was on her schoolwork. They both had that in common. Not only was Michael a triathlete, but he also had the third-highest GPA in the school.

Michael was a junior and already had college scouts coming to his games in track, baseball, and basketball. He stood at six five with a wingspan of six ten. Michael just turned seventeen years old and had the recruiters going wild with their predictions of how much he would grow over the upcoming season, barring any injuries. Michael was also a coach's dream. He was hard-working, listened to feedback, and was able to execute the coach's direction almost instantaneously. He was also a great teammate and loved to play just as much as he loved to win.

"Of course, we're gonna be there...everybody's gonna be there," Althea replied, trying to look flirty as she twirled her sandy brown hair that was already curled around her red-tipped fingers.

"Ummm...well, Mike, I guess we'll see you tonight then," Shaunice said shyly, barely looking up at Michael. But Shaunice knew her parents would never let her go to a basketball game on a Wednesday night. Wednesday nights were reserved for prayer meeting and Bible study.

Michael reluctantly walked away because the bell sounded. "Can I walk you to class, Shaunny?'

"We always walk to fourth period!" Althea almost cried out like a toddler throwing a tantrum.

Shaunice stood with her mouth open, stuck, not knowing who to choose: her best friend since they were kids, or her first crush. Shaunice knew how unforgiving Althea could be. Once Shaunice could not make it to Althea's twelfth birthday party at the skating rink because her grandmother was in the hospital and Althea never forgave her for it. Shaunice had to practically beg and grovel for Althea's forgiveness. Shaunice was not ready to relive that humiliation again so soon.

Michael saw the pain and struggle in Shaunice's eyes. "It's okay, Shaunny, walk with your girl, I'll see you tonight." And with that, Michael gave Shaunice a sweet peck on the cheek and quickly took his leave.

Shaunice turned around, fighting a squeal that she knew would reverberate off the walls. She was in heaven! One of the most popular and interesting boys at school liked her. He really liked her! *Oh, my goodness I can't believe it!* Shaunice thought as she floated down the hallway. "I wonder what I should wear. Oh, I know! My new white body suit and jean bibs. That would look so fly. I think I will sit right in the front so Mike can see me." Her inner monologue was now pouring out of her mouth. She'd forgotten that she was walking, let alone beside Althea.

"Don't you have church tonight?" Althea blurted out behind Shaunice, interrupting her thoughts.

Shaunice almost didn't hear Althea's words because she was so consumed by her own excitement.

Althea cleared her throat, "Ummm, Shaunice," she said with authority. "Don't you have church tonight? Remember, it's Wednesday?"

Shaunice stutter stepped as Althea's words penetrated her momentary happiness. "Oh…yeah. I forgot." She sighed with disappointment.

"Well, maybe your mom will let you go tonight," Althea said with fake concern in her voice. She knew as well as Shaunice did that her parents would never let her miss Wednesday night service for a basketball game. The two girls walked in silence to their fourth period. The rest of the afternoon was a blur for Shaunice.

The night came and went, and as usual, Shaunice found herself at church. The next day the school was electric due to the win the basketball team had clinched. Shaunice stood at her locker gathering her books for first through third period. Shaunice was still bummed about missing the game and her opportunity to lock eyes with Mike and cheer him on to victory. She was slowly getting her books and notes together when whispering voices from down the hall grew louder as they neared. Shaunice looked up and saw Michael walking toward her, giving high fives to people in the hallway. Then she noticed a girl on his arm. Not any girl, but her best friend…Althea! Michael walked down the hallway with his arm around Althea's neck while she enjoyed every eye focusing on her. She walked in sync with Michael while twirling her hair around her finger and chewing bubble gum.

Shaunice's eyes narrowed and focused on her best friend's face. She could not believe what she saw. The absolute heartbreak that she felt took her breath away, and she had to steady herself against her locker as the new couple walked by her, oblivious to her presence. Shaunice closed her locker and ran to the bathroom with tears streaming down her face. She closed the door to the stall and sobbed. She felt like she couldn't catch her breath. She kept repeating to herself, "Why would she do that...why would she do that?"

Shaunice heard the bell ring for first period and waited about ten minutes, washed her faced, and headed to the nurse's office. She told the nurse that she didn't feel well and needed to call her mother and have her pick her up from school. Shaunice really was sick: sick to her stomach that her best friend would betray her like that. Althea knew how much she liked Mike; she knew because he was all she talked about. "How could she do that to me?"

Althea looked for Shaunice in second period science, but she didn't show up. Althea had her excuse practiced and ready to go, but her best friend was a no-show. Althea noticed that Shaunice was a no-show for third period as well and began to feel a pang of guilt. However, that guilt was quickly erased when Michael showed up at her locker and all the girls in the vicinity gave her an envious look. Althea gave them a grin and wrapped her arm around Michael's tall, thin frame and walked to class. The attention she was getting far outweighed the guilt she felt. She rationalized that Shaunice didn't know what to do with a man like Michael anyway. *It's not like she would be able to go to any of his games. She's a church girl.* Althea thought. *And if she really wanted him, she should've fought for him. I know I would've.* She smirked as she looked up into Michael's face while he escorted her to gym class.

Althea was on a high all day after bottom-feeding off the attention of the other teenage girls in her high school like a parasite enjoying their host. They hated Althea! They hated her long hair, her hazel eyes, and her fresh clothes. But most of all they hated Althea's attitude because she was rude and thought she was better than everyone. It wasn't that she lived in a nicer house; she had a false sense of superiority that Mother Rose drilled into her day after day.

"Make sure you pack yo' bag and I'm gonna give you some money for you and Shaunny to get pizza and skate," Mother Rose ordered Althea.

Mother Rose had a three-city run tomorrow, and, as usual, she told Althea to pack her bag and go over to Shaunice's house while she was out of town. Mother Rose said it effortlessly and didn't give a second thought that Althea was no longer welcome at Shaunice's house while she had to "work." Mother Rose had been dropping Althea off at Gwen's for as long as she could remember. Shaunice and Gwen were the only family that Althea knew because Mother Rose alienated her blood relatives one by one because of her scheming ways. Mother Rose had put utility bills in family members' names, cashed checks in her sister's name, and stole the identity of her mother and grandmother to conduct fraudulent wire transfers and tax fraud. Mother Rose's family wanted absolutely nothing to do with her. Althea was really the only family that had not totally abandoned her. Mother Rose knew this and kept buying Althea's love because she really didn't know what love was, nor how to reciprocate it.

Althea looked at her feet and said in a low voice, "We ain't friends no more."

"What?" Mother Rose whipped her head around in disbelief.

"Yeah...we ain't friends no more. Shaunny got mad that a boy liked me instead of her." Althea shrugged her shoulders as she lied.

In fact, it was Althea who approached Michael after the game and asked him if he was going to "the spot" afterward. Michael said that yes, he was going, but he was looking behind Althea for Shaunice but she wasn't there. "Oh, she went to the bathroom," Althea lied. She knew she had to get Michael alone and he would never willingly meet her after the game instead of Shaunice.

So, she broke Michael's concentration by poking her chest out a little bit further so that her full C-cup breasts would push the top of her pink-laced bra to the top of her bodysuit; she knew how to get a high school boy's attention. Michael agreed to meet her there.

Althea spent the rest of the night kissing Michael and letting him finger her, making him forget all about boring, church girl Shaunny.

"Forget about her, you don't need her, she was probably jealous of you anyway, baby," said Mother Rose, assuming Althea was sad about her friendship with Shaunice. "She's always been jealous of your clothes and shoes. And you know she always wanna judge...her and her Mama. You're old enough to stay home now by yourself anyway. We don't need them."

Mother Rose and Shaunice's mother, Gwen, grew up together. They were childhood friends until Mother Rose dropped out of school in the ninth grade and began living a fast-paced lifestyle leading nowhere. While on the other hand, Shaunice's mother, Gwen, finished high school and became a licensed practical nurse and married her high school sweetheart. Gwen and her husband did not have the perfect marriage, but they loved each other and tried to raise Shaunice in a loving environment. Shaunice's dad was a deacon at the church and received a small salary. Gwen was the breadwinner in the family and paid most of the bills. Mother Rose was right about one thing: Gwen did look down on Mother Rose's lifestyle because it was centered around materialistic things. Gwen also saw Althea going in the same direction as Mother Rose. That's why Gwen always let Althea spend the night when Mother Rose went on one of her two-to-three-day boosting runs. Gwen wanted to show Althea a normal, loving household and that normal and boring can also be a fulfilling and rich lifestyle. However, when Shaunice came home and cried her eyes out because of Althea's betrayal, she knew that Althea was lost. Gwen had to put her daughter first. She was her number one priority.

While Althea was telling Mother Rose that Shaunice and she were no longer friends, Shaunice was just waking up after binge-crying all day. Her mother was concerned when she got a phone call from the school to pick Shaunice up. She knew she had to call in and take the day off from work. Gwen could see that her daughter had been crying when she signed her out at the highs school's main office. Gwen didn't want to push Shaunice to talk, so she gave enough silence and space for her daughter to naturally open up. By the time they made it to the driveway, Shaunice began to cry again and told her mother about seeing Althea with her crush in the hallway. They sat in the car for a long while as Shaunice cried to her mother and voiced all her confusion and outrage. Then, when Gwen felt her daughter expressed all her feelings, she thought to offer her wisdom.

Gwen told Shaunice in a sweet, loving voice, "Sometimes the ones we love most, hurt us the deepest." Shaunice began to sob harder as her mother's words sunk in. All Gwen could do was rub her daughter's back while she helplessly watched her heart break, right there in her lap. Gwen hated seeing her daughter suffer.

"I am so sorry this happened to you, baby girl." Gwen whispered softly into Shaunice's ear as she continued to gently stroke her back. Shaunice's violent sobs turned to sniffles and Gwen instinctively knew that her daughter would be okay. She gently coaxed her daughter out of the car and urged her to take a nap and reassured her that everything would make sense in the morning.

"I don't ever want to see her again, Mom," Shaunice whispered. Gwen nodded. She knew there was no salvaging Shaunice and Althea's friendship.

"I know, baby, but you're going to have to see her. You don't have to deal with her, but you will eventually see her. It's up to you how you handle it. You give people power when they make you act out of character. So, let's figure out how you're going to handle it."

Shaunice nodded. They worked out a plan for how to handle Althea. They agreed the best course of action would be to make a clean cut from Althea and stopping all communication. They talked all night to work out how the friendship breakup would look. Gwen and Shaunice figured out every angle that Althea would try to leverage and manipulate Shaunice back into the one-sided friendship. But Shaunice was determined that she wouldn't give her traitor-best friend an opportunity to apologize or make it up to her. In fact, Shaunice decided that she would no longer give Althea access to her at all. She decided that any conversation could be used to sway her and remind Shaunice of the good times Althea and she had had. She knew she had to remain obstinate in her convictions to not give Althea a foothold in her life ever again. After talking with her mother all night, Shaunice discovered Althea's kryptonite. Althea loved attention, and the greatest way to hurt Althea would be to ignore her.

The next morning Shaunice woke up and saw the indicator on her cordless phone showing three voicemails. Shaunice quickly deleted the voicemails without listening to them. Hearing Althea's voice made her stomach churn in knots. Shaunice slowly swung her feet out of bed and placed them on the floor as a means of grounding. While she took a deep breath, she had to remind herself that the day before was not a dream and her life was forever changed without the presence of her best friend.

Meanwhile, a few blocks away, Althea woke up to an empty house. Mother Rose left the night before on her boosting trip. Althea looked at her answering machine notifying her she had zero messages.

Althea got dressed for the day. She decided on a casual look. She chose baggy, light denim jeans with a white body suit and a red plaid shirt tied around her waist. She styled her outfit with some large hoop earrings and combat boots. Then she felt like gaining a little extra attention and threw on a chained belt with charms on it, adding a girly pop to her outfit. Althea jumped in her 1990 fire-engine red Volkswagen Jetta that she begged Mother Rose for when she got her permit the year before. Althea loved pulling up to the school in her Jetta at just the right time so that more people would see her; it always gave her a boost.

She usually stopped by Shaunice's house, no matter how late or early she was running; Althea knew Shaunice was waiting. Out of habit, Althea drove by Shaunice's house and to her surprise, no Shaunice. *I wonder where she is,* Althea thought, almost forgetting the hurt look in her best friend's eyes the day before. Althea shrugged and turned the corner to continue the short drive to school.

Although it was in middle of winter in the Midwest, a group of students still gathered outside talking before the first bell rang. She saw Michael there with the other jocks in a group, all gathered with their letterman jackets on. She saw Michael's head whip around and smile when he saw Althea pull into her assigned parking spot. Althea instinctively rolled her eyes, forgetting Michael was supposed to be her new boyfriend. He was the most desirable guy in school, and she was supposed to be ecstatic that he'd chosen her out of all the other girls to walk arm-in-arm with down the hallway. But she wasn't ecstatic at all; she was actually bored with all of the high school rites of passage, like having a boyfriend on a sports team or being a cheerleader. These things were beneath Althea. She couldn't wait to graduate so she could go on the road with Mother Rose and learn the ins and outs of how to "get money". Her mother's lifestyle seemed exciting, plus, she hated being left home alone in a quiet house.

Althea went through her day avoiding the puppy-like following of Michael. He was at her locker or her classes, seemingly before the bell rang, to escort her to her next class. Althea usually walked with Shaunice during passing periods but noted Shaunice wasn't at school that day. Althea started to feel guilty until her thoughts were interrupted.

"Hey, baby, let me carry your bookbag to gym," Michael offered.

"Oh...thanks." Althea gave a weak smile. "Have you seen Shaunice today?"

"Ummm...no, and after last night, I ain't checking for her either. She ain't even my speed anyway, you know church girls never give it up."

"Hold the fuck up!" Althea was offended. "What's that supposed to mean? And I do?

"Naw...well...I mean," Michael stuttered. He didn't know what to say. Althea had let him do almost everything but penetrate her last night in his car while they were parked behind the school after the game.

"You know what?" Althea stopped short of cussing Michael out and stormed off to her next class instead. Althea sat in the bleachers instead of participating in gym. She felt so stupid that she had betrayed her best friend, thinking Michael thought she was better than Shaunice when really Michael chose the girl he thought was the easiest.

CHAPTER ELEVEN

WHO NEEDS ENEMIES

Althea decided to go to Shaunice's house after school to apologize for how selfish she had been. When she arrived, Shaunice's mother met Althea at the gate to their house. "Hey, Althea, Shaunice isn't going to be riding with you anymore to or from school. And I've already talked to your mother about finding another option for you when she goes out of town," Gwen said evenly.

Althea was so puzzled; she didn't know what to say and couldn't believe her ears. She knew that Shaunice may have been upset about Michael, but she didn't think anything, or anyone for that matter, would ever come between them.

"So, what are you saying, she doesn't wanna hang out anymore?" Althea was so confused.

"No, sweetie, she doesn't want to hang out anymore...she doesn't even want to be friends." Shaunice's mother was trying to be gentle because, at the end of the day, Althea was still a child. "Like I said before, I already spoke with Mother Rose about it. You should talk to her if you have any other questions."

"But I don't understand what happened. What did I do to make her not wanna be my friend no more?" Althea pleaded.

"Well, Althea, I know that Shaunice was very hurt when you went out with a boy that you knew she liked. I think it just hurt her so much that she doesn't feel like she can trust you anymore." Shaunice's Mom came closer to Althea because she could see the tears welling up in her eyes. "Look, baby, I know you and Shaunice have been friends since even before I can remember, but it's over. I'm sorry, sweetie." Shaunice's Mom reluctantly turned away. She knew her house was the only haven for Althea, but she had to think of her daughter first. Shaunice no longer wanted to be friends with Althea and there was nothing Shaunice's Mom could say or do to change that. She raised her daughter to think for herself. She also taught Shaunice not to let anyone mistreat her.

Althea sank into the seat of her car in a heap. She put her car in reverse and drove a few houses down to hers. She was in a daze as she climbed out of her car and opened the front gate. When she got inside Mother Rose was sitting on the couch smoking a cigarette with her legs crossed, bouncing one leg on top of the other.

"So, I see you talked to that bitch, Gwen!" Althea's mother spat out as she stood and began pacing the living room while taking a long drag from her cigarette. "I never liked that uppity bitch, she always think her and her raggedy ass daughter's better than everyone. I knew I shouldn't let you go over there from the start." Mother Rose continued to ramble. "That bitch act like she love you so much and care for you! Lying ass!"

Mother Rose continued to pace back and forth while puffing on her cigarette, bracelets jangling with every movement.

"And who the hell supposed to watch you while I go on the road? I was supposed to leave earlier until that bitch came over talkn' bout you ain't welcome at her house." Mother Rose was talking more to herself at that moment than to her daughter.

Althea stood still, trying to process that Shaunice and she were no longer friends. No more sleepovers. No more nights filled with giggles. No more shared scary stories. No more of Ms. Gwen's famous chocolate chip cookies. She felt absolutely lost. She didn't realize that she was standing still with her mouth open until Mother Rose started talking again.

"And what the hell's wrong wit you over there looking all lost and shit? I been told you that you can't trust nobody in this world. The sooner you realize that the better off you gonna be."

"But Shaunny is my friend, we grew up together," Althea whined.

"Well, you see she ain't thankn' 'bout 'yo lil' ass now, is she? And another thang...Gwen told me that ya'll fell out behind some little knotty head lil' boy at ya'll school."

Mother Rose stopped and cocked her head to the side, staring at Althea and waiting for an answer. After a long silence Mother Rose rolled her eyes. "So, it's true...I thought Gwen's ass was lying. I told her that no way my baby girl would ever let some knucklehead come between ya'll. But by the look on yo' face, I guess I was wrong. What was you thankn' Thea?"

"I don't know," Althea replied and shrugged.

"Now I know damn well, there are other boys in that damn school, and you know Shaunny's ass ain't no kinda special, so why wouldn't you just let her have one...huh? Just one boy."

Mother Rose just shook her head. "And I told you about worrying about them boys anyways. Well...I gotta go outta town this weekend on one of my runs. I was planning on leaving for four days, but I guess I gotta hurry back to watch yo' fast ass huh?"

Althea sighed and started to walk to her room with her bookbag hanging off her arm. All she could think about was Shaunny and how she didn't even want to come to the door and tell her how she felt. *Was she that bad of a friend?* Althea wondered. She decided to lie down and take a nap because her head was pounding and she knew there wasn't anything in the cabinets or the fridge for a snack. All she wanted to do was sleep.

Althea woke up to a start. It was pitch black in her room and she could hear the blues coming from their stereo in the living room. She could hear her mother giggling and the muffled sounds of a man's voice. She knew Mother Rose had company, and she also knew better than to come out of her room. Althea remembered she had stashed a bag of chips and a soda in her bag right before fourth period. She planned to have her snack at Shaunny's house while they did their homework. Just the thought of Shaunice made Althea's stomach slightly churn. Her best friend...gone. Who would she hang out with now? Althea never bothered to get to know any of the other girls in high school, or in middle school for that matter. Shaunice had been her best friend since they were toddlers.

Althea started to eat her snack and turned on her TV to see what was on. Then she heard the door to her mother's bedroom shut, so she scurried to use the bathroom. She knew Mother Rose and her company wouldn't be coming out anytime soon, but she didn't want to make the mistake of running into whatever man Mother Rose chose to be her company for the night. She shuddered thinking of what happened the last time she ran into one of Mother Rose's "friends."

The next day Althea woke up feeling groggy and a slight headache lingered from the stress of the day before. As she got dressed, she wondered what her day would be like. Who would she sit with at lunch and who would she talk to during passing periods?

As Althea pulled up to the school, she checked her lip gloss in her rearview mirror. She looked cute that day despite all the chaos going on in her life. She sat in her car, acting as if she had something important to do when she was really waiting for the first bell to ring so she could go straight to her first period class. Althea looked for Shaunice all day but didn't see her. Althea thought that maybe Shaunice didn't come to school until she saw her at the other end of the hallway going up another set of stairs opposite from the route they usually took together. *Dang,* Althea thought. Shaunice was at school; she was just avoiding Althea. Lunch time came, but it wasn't as brutal without Shaunice as Althea imagined. Althea saw a group of football players sitting at a table and decided to join them. Her ego was bruised, and she needed a quick pick-me-up. The football players always gave her the attention she craved. The rest of the day droned on as normal. As Althea drove home, she saw Shaunice and her mother getting out of the car in front of Shaunice's house. She didn't even look in Althea's direction. She hurried inside to avoid making eye contact.

Althea came home to a quiet house as usual. She found a note from Mother Rose on the small kitchen table. It said that she left to make her run and she would be back in a few days. Mother Rose left two $100 bills on the table for Althea. All she could do was sigh with relief: at least she would have the small house to herself for a few days while she sorted out all this stuff with Shaunice.

Althea never knew how long Mother Rose's runs would last. Sometimes she would be gone for a weekend, and other times she would be gone four to five days. She thought she remembered hearing Mother Rose talking to one of her regulars from St. Louis saying she would be there after first hitting Chicago. So, she figured Mother Rose shouldn't be gone any longer than three days. But she knew to use the $200 very sparingly, just in case Mother Rose took longer than expected. Plus, Althea always had a little cash stashed away in her room in case she needed it.

Althea decided she would go to the grocery store first thing in the morning before school so no one would see her and ask too many questions concerning the whereabouts of Mother Rose. She didn't want to ask any questions or even be polite to any of Mother Rose's clients. She didn't have the energy.

Chapter Twelve

FIGHT OR FLIGHT

Three days passed and still no Mother Rose. Althea wasn't worried, she figured Mother Rose got caught up with one of her "friends" in Chicago, St. Louis, or somewhere between. Since it was Saturday night, Althea thought she would go and hang out at the skating rink. It was open until one a.m. and everybody who was anybody would be there. For as long as Althea could remember, Mother Rose had been dropping her off while she made her "runs." Althea grew to love roller skating because she could show off her latest fashions while floating and bopping to the music, escaping a reality of abandonment. Plus, she could eat cheaply and take home a few pizza slices for the next day's breakfast. She had a well-thought plan to look so fly no one would question her about Mother Rose or Shaunice.

Althea readied herself for the rink and brushed her shoulder length, sandy-brown hair into a ponytail so whoever was looking could see her custom door-knocker earrings that said *Love* on one side and *Thea* on the other. She decided on her favorite low-rise, button-fly, light blue jeans and dark blue button-up belly shirt, complete with a belly chain that would look perfect under the strobe lights of the rink. She decided to complete her look with a bright orange lipstick because it glowed in the black lights at the rink. She made sure to stuff some money into her pockets and hide the remaining $200 in her stash spot just in case someone was watching the house. Mother Rose taught her to never leave valuables out to tempt a thief.

Althea liked to cruise the parking lot before going inside, making sure there were enough people present to see her make an entrance, but she usually had Shaunny there with her to make fun of people to pass the time. She felt a little embarrassed to be at the skating rink alone. When she pulled up to the parking lot, it was packed. There were a few people she recognized from her school hanging out in the parking lot. She noticed the group of wannabe ballers under a streetlamp in one corner of the parking lot. They never came inside, they just smoked weed and held rap cyphers. Althea rolled her eyes thinking of them all huddled together spitting in each other's faces and exchanging stale weed breath. She saw the cars of a few of the regulars who were there every Friday and Saturday for open skate night, so she felt more comfortable and less alone. The skating rink was a second home to her, besides Shaunice's house, and once she stepped inside, she felt like a local celebrity.

As she made her way inside with her skates thrown over her shoulder, Althea could hear the cat-calls from the weed corner of the parking lot. She knew she made the right choice in her ensemble. She just smirked and continued to walk and chew on her gum as she reveled in the attention. Once she got inside, she could feel the electricity of the skate rink. She quickly found an empty locker, put her skates on, and hit the floor. Althea liked to see who was in the building from the rink floor. As she made her first lap, she saw the girls from her school frown at her as she skated by, and she made sure to switch her ass extra hard in her jeans. Then she skated over to the DJ's booth to let him know she was there. The DJ was an old family friend. Mother Rose told Althea if she were ever in trouble Jack was the one to go to. He looked out for Althea like she were his little sister, since he was only five years older than her. "Hey, Jack!" Althea screamed over the music.

"Thee-Thee, what up, girl?" Jack called back and pointed at Althea. Jack already knew that Althea wanted to hear some slow grinding R&B and some of those hits coming outta the West Coast. Jack was one of the baddest DJs in the city; he always played what was new and upcoming since the small midwestern town they were in didn't have any radio stations that played predominantly black music. All that was played over the air waves was light rock and pop.

Althea circled around the rink a few times, peeping the scene: seeing who was coupled up, who was trying to talk to a girl, and who was there trying to flaunt their money. Althea thought she'd seen everyone who was at the rink for the moment, so she decided to take a break and get a snack. As she sat down with her soda and nachos with extra cheese and jalapeños, she heard an unfamiliar voice come from above her.

"Can I have a bite?" A deep voice cut through the booming music so close to Althea's ear that she could feel warm breath on her neck and ear. Althea jumped at the closeness and deepness of the stranger's voice.

"Oh, I'm sorry if I scared you," the smooth voice said again before Althea could turn around and see who dared to invade her private space. Althea was ready to cuss whoever this was up, down, and around the skating rink, but once she saw the face that the voice came from, she sat mid-nacho, stuck in silence. The man slid into the bench across the picnic table from Althea with the biggest, whitest smile she'd ever seen in her life. He unashamedly looked Althea deep into her eyes, still smiling and holding her gaze. She was still at a loss for words because this was a man who clearly was not from her small city. He had on a distressed jean jacket with the word *dope* airbrushed repeatedly across the front and a fresh white T-shirt underneath. His skin was deep chocolate and smooth, not a blemish in sight. He was clean-shaven with a low fade. That smile and those lips, Althea squirmed in her seat a little while the stranger continued his silent appreciation of what he saw before him. He had 360 waves on this thick, dark hair that was lined to perfection. Althea took a sip of her soda because she still didn't know what to say. The usual nasty attitude she had with guys who tried to approach her alluded her at that moment.

As she took a sip, Althea noticed the smaller details that Mother Rose taught her to pay attention to. So, Althea looked at the stranger's fingernails. *Hmmm...clean and manicured,* she thought. *So, he can't do any hard labor and they look soft,* Althea thought to herself. Then, she noticed the earrings in both ears, not too big, not to small. The way the earrings glittered in this light; Althea bet her life the diamonds were real. Then she noticed the pinky ring on his left finger had a diamond encrusted *D* on it. Althea took a moment to soak in all the stranger's handsome glory but feigned annoyance, finished her soda, and bobbed her head to the music. The stranger wasn't fazed by Althea ignoring him. He grinned and locked eyes on her.

Althea puffed. "So, what does the *D* stand for? Dickhead?" She motioned toward his pinky ring while still pretending she was drinking her soda.

"So, what's your name?" The stranger completely ignored Althea's smart comment. He sat patiently, waiting for her reply adjusting his pinky ring with the biggest smile on his face.

"T.T." Althea lied. She never gave her real name out to strangers.

"For real?" The stranger said matter-of-factly and reached in and grabbed one of Althea's cheesy nachos.

"Ummm, excuse you, greedy! Nobody said you could have any of my nachos!" Althea was pissed. Who did this guy think he was? Just coming over and inviting himself to her table and now her nachos!

The stranger just continued to smile at her. When he finished chewing, he said, "That's not what I heard."

"Not what you heard?" Althea had a major attitude now, neck and eyes rolling.

"I heard your name was Althea." The stranger sat back and let the information sink in that he knew her name, but she didn't have a clue as to his identity.

Althea sighed, rolled her neck and eyes at the same time. Now she was annoyed at the stranger. At first glance she was really attracted to him, but now that he acted like a know-it-all, she was completely turned off. She resumed eating her nachos and looking at the skaters. She hoped he would get the hint that she was no longer interested in having a conversation with him and leave the table out of sheer embarrassment, but no such luck. The stranger just sat there and continued with a huge smile.

"I asked about you," the stranger finally confessed. "Yeah, I saw you talking to the DJ and asked him who you were," the stranger answered with a smile.

Now Althea was livid. This was so out of character for Jack; he knew better than to talk to guys about her. She was curious about what was so special about this stranger that Jack felt comfortable giving her real name to him.

She whipped her long ponytail around. "Who...Jack?"

"Yeah, I asked him what your name was, and he told me. That's all I needed to know. I wanted to find out the rest for myself."

Althea sucked her teeth and looked directly at the stranger. "Well, you came and saw." She cocked her head to the left, swung her ponytail again, and rolled her hazel eyes. She was not gonna make it easy for him. Her nacho cheese had grown cold and now she was irritated and ready to leave the rink, but not before she checked Jack. She started to get up to leave, and the stranger stood and quickly moved to her side.

"Lemme throw that away for you." The stranger quickly grabbed the tray.

Althea couldn't help but notice how tall the stranger was. He loomed over her, even with her skates on, with such a big grin on his face, it almost disarmed Althea once again. He had to be a least six four, she assumed. "Thanks," Althea begrudgingly offered. Before the stranger could utter another word, Althea was off on her skates, hitting the roller rink floor. Her head was spinning with thoughts. *Who in the heck was this dude and who did he think he was?* Althea was always leery of over-friendly men. Her mother taught her that men only wanted two things from a woman: sex and to get over. Althea didn't have plans of either happening.

She skated around the roller rink three times to clear her head before remembering that she had to check Jack, so on her third time around, she rolled in the DJ's booth. Althea cocked her head and stared at Jack. He was expecting this unwelcomed interaction all night. "Heyyy, cuz," Jack stammered.

"Ain't no 'hey, cuz!' Why you give that dude my name? I don't know him, and he sure don't know me. Wait 'til I tell Mother Rose that you been giving out my name to strangers," Althea threatened.

"Now, wait, cuz, ain't no need to go and tell Mother Rose. The man gave me $200 just for me to tell him your name. He said he ain't want nothing else." Jack quickly pulled out the two crisp $100 bills. Althea snatched one of the $100 bills.

"And this is for making sure I don't tell Mother Rose because you know she don't play." Althea glared at Jack and stood silent, waiting for him to protest, but he knew she was right. He didn't have any reason to give out Althea's real name to a stranger.

Althea's face softened a little. "Look, I won't tell Mother Rose about this, but you gotta be more careful. You know Mother Rose has competition and enemies out here in these streets and we don't know all of them. Could be somebody wanting to hurt me to get to her. You gotta think, bruh." Althea gave Jack a quick hug to let him know she wasn't going to stay mad. "But Imma still keep this bill though." Althea laughed and skated away.

The night was winding down, so Althea thought it would be a great time to make her exit just in case the stranger or anyone who was with him was waiting for her to leave. Althea got her shoes out of her locker and went behind the counter of the shoe rental. There was a side exit to the skating rink that only employees used. She always parked her car by this exit just in case a fight broke out or someone decided to shoot up the place, which was rather frequent. Althea paused and poked her head out the door to make sure there was no one by her car and that she wasn't being watched or followed. She made a quick dash to her car when she heard the stranger's voice.

"So, you just gonna leave without saying goodbye?" He was leaning on the hood of his all-back Lexus, rims shining, bass bumping. "I said, so, you just gonna leave without saying goodbye?" the stranger repeated, not giving Althea a chance to even get her head all the way out of the door.

Althea thought to herself that all she needed to do was make her way to her car where she carried a small.22, but she didn't know the stranger's intentions or if someone else was watching, so she dug her hand in her purse to locate her box cutter. Mother Rose taught her to always have a weapon on her in case some jealous girl tried her. Althea fiddled around in her purse looking for her box cutter while partially hiding behind the door.

"What you want from me?" Althea yelled aggressively. She no longer found the stranger's pursuits funny or welcoming. *There,* Althea thought she found her box cutter as she slid it up, all the while looking behind the stranger to make sure no one was watching them and waiting for an opportunity to strike. The stranger didn't move from his spot, so Althea made her move to her car. She quickly made it inside and started her car.

The stranger moved to her passenger side window and bent down and smiled. "Look, let's start over again. My name is Diamond, I saw you in there and you were the most beautiful girl I've seen since I moved here about a month ago. Honestly, I just wanna know if I can get to know you, that's all. Not trying to hurt you, baby girl."

He looks sincere enough, Althea thought. But she couldn't be too sure. She paused for a moment and then heard Mother Rose's voice in her head saying, *A man don't want nothing from you except what's between your legs or to use you. You use that motherfucker first!* Althea's curiosity got the best of her though. She wanted to know the stranger's motives for trying to get next to her.

"Well, I am kinda hungry," Althea told Diamond and batted her eyes. "We could go to the McDonald's down the road. That's where everybody goes after skating."

"Oh, okay" Diamond wagered his next words carefully. "Well, I really want to get to know you, Althea. I wanna sit down and talk, not be interrupted by a bunch of noise."

Althea liked this approach. She liked feeling special, but she still didn't know if she could trust this handsome face in front of her. "So, where are you thinking instead?"

"Well, there's an old truck stop on the edge of town I ate at a few times. The food is good and it's quiet." Diamond quickly looked at Althea's face to gauge what she was thinking about his proposal.

The truck stop, she thought. The same truck stop that one of Mother's Rose's favorite customers owned and operated. Althea knew that she would be safe there because Ms. Channel would look out for her and not let any funny business happen on her watch. "Okay, that's what's up. I could go for a T-bone and eggs right about now," Althea replied. She thought that the word *T-bone* would automatically turn Diamond off if he were a cheapskate.

"Yeah, a T-bone does sound good. I may have one, too," Diamond replied. "And just to make sure you don't try and dip off into traffic, I'm gonna let you hold something just to make sure you gonna come and not ditch me," Diamond said with a huge smile. He reached into his pocket and pulled out a wad of cash. He flipped it open so Althea could see it was mostly hundreds, fifties, and twenties. He peeled off $400 and handed it to her. "So, I'll follow you there, right?"

Althea looked at the $400, raised her eyebrow, and took the money through the passenger winder. "See you there." Althea quickly put her car in reverse and peeled out of the parking lot, dodging people and laughing out loud. She just made $500 off this man in one night; now she regretted not letting Jack keep the other $100. Althea zoomed down the street, thrilled by the money Diamond willingly handed over. One thing she knew for sure was that he wasn't cheap! *But wait...*Althea thought. *I don't know anything else about him. I don't know his last name, his first name, where he lives, or what he did to make that fat wad of cash. Was he attracted to young girls? Was he a* *serial killer?* That last thought alone sent a chill down Althea's spine: thinking about all the horror stories Mother Rose told her about her early days of hooking and how girls would get picked up and never seen or heard from again. She had to be smart, she told herself. She resolved to still her feelings of excitement and intrigue. Althea rode in silence on the way to the truck stop, formulating a plan to get to know Diamond and his motives.

Althea got to the truck stop first and went inside. Ms. Channel immediately saw her and greeted Althea with a big hug. Ms. Channel was the first transwoman Althea ever knew, but she never treated Ms. Channel as anything other than what she was, which was a ghetto-fabulous woman. Ms. Channel waitressed and owned the truck stop. She also hooked on the side with repeat trucker customers who loved spending time with a woman like Ms. Channel in a judgment-free zone. She kept herself in all the latest fashions and never wore a uniform to hide her fabulous outfits, complete with hair and makeup. Ms. Channel lived her life out, loud, and proud! The men who came to the truck stop knew Ms. Channel as a national landmark. She always made the men feel at home and eased their loneliness after being out on the road for days at a time.

"Hey baby, how you doin'?" Ms. Channel greeted Althea with a large hug and kiss on the cheek when she saw her. "I gotta spot right over here at the counter for you, baby," Ms. Channel said in her always cheerful tone.

"Oh, ummm...I got somebody meeting me here tonight, Ms. Channel. Can I have a table?" Althea whispered and kept her eyes low to avoid the peering curiosity of Ms. Channel.

"You meeting Mother Rose? I thought she was on a run because I showed her a piece that I wanted out of the latest fashion magazine, and I know she was on the hunt."

"Yeah, she's still outta town. I'm meeting someone here," Althea said sheepishly.

Ms. Channel eyed Althea suspiciously. "Well, I'm gonna put ya'll in my section just to keep an eye on you. You know it's too late for you to be out in these damn streets this late at night and Mother Rose ain't nowhere around. You know what they say, ain't nothing but trouble and legs open after midnight, little girl." Ms. Channel gave a quick humph, pursed her lips, and sat Althea in a booth near the window.

Just as she was being seated, Diamond showed up, towering over Ms. Channel. "Hey, I could barely keep up with you." Diamond tried to sit, but Ms. Channel turned her full body away from Althea and blocked his entrance into the booth.

"So, what's your name, young man? And how old are you and what you want with my Thea?" Ms. Channel asked in a threatening tone, almost losing her sweet quality and inserting bass to let Diamond know she was not to be toyed with. Diamond looked at Ms. Channel and scoffed at her, He tried to sit until Ms. Chanel shifted her weight and the whole diner got quiet and turned their heads toward the commotion. Everyone in the diner knew to respect Ms. Channel, and they would go to blows with anyone who disrespected her.

Diamond could feel the tension in the diner and all the eyes on him. "Yes, ma'am, my name is Jerod Rose, but everyone calls me Diamond. I'm nineteen years old and just moved here from the city a few months ago with my grandmother."

"And what you want with my Thea? You know she only sixteen, right?" Ms. Channel said with a twist of her neck. The diner was still silent, waiting for Diamond's answer.

"Yes, ma'am, I only want to get to know her better is all. I thought she was really pretty when I first saw her. I talked to her for a minute at the skating rink and just wanted to sit down and talk where it was quieter." Diamond now began to visibly develop sweat beads on his forehead because he was so nervous from the aggressive way Ms. Channel was acting. "Well, let me just tell you, son, I don't play about my Thea and neither do Mother Rose. Now, you think I'm tough, you ain't seen nothing. Now, what can I get you to drink? I'll bring ya'll some water. Thea, you want a shake to start?" Ms. Channel didn't even wait for Althea to confirm, she just nodded, gave Diamond a disapproving look, and walked away. The whole diner began buzzing again when Ms. Channel left to get their drink orders.

"So, Jerod, huh?" Althea said with a slight smirk on her face. She thought, *he looks nothing like a Jerod.*

"Diamond is good," he said with a laugh that was a little too loud and filled with nervous energy. "So, is that your aunt or something?"

"Naw, Ms. Channel is just one of Mother Rose's best customers," Althea relayed.

"So, who exactly is Mother Rose? Is that like your godmother or something?

"No." Althea laughed. "That's my mom. Everyone calls her Mother Rose."

"Where is she? She's not gonna come running outta the kitchen with a butcher knife or something, is she?" Diamond half-laughed and looked over his shoulder to be sure. Althea thought him being scared was kind of cute.

"No, she's not gonna come outta the kitchen. But enough about her, what about you? You live with your grandma?"

"Yeah, she raised me since I was three years old. We moved from up north because she said I was moving too fast. She got a house through Section 8 and a program for seniors, and we moved here a few months ago." Diamond was so free with his information. Althea instantly felt comfortable around him and nestled into her booth a little more and relaxed.

Just then, Ms. Channel came back with Althea's shake and two waters. "So, what ya'll gonna have?"

"I'm gonna take the steak and eggs, hash browns, and a side of fried mushrooms to start. And please don't forget that horseradish sauce I love," Althea rattled off.

"Yeah, that sounds good. I'll have a T-bone, eggs, and home fries," Diamond smiled and gave Ms. Channel his menu. "Oh, can I also have some hot tea, too, please? And before I go, I want to place an order to take home to my grandma."

Ms. Channel couldn't help but gush over Diamond ordering something for his grandmother. "Awe...look at you, now ain't you just the sweetest thang?" Ms. Channel cooed and walked away with a skip in her step. About five seconds later, she was back with Althea's mushrooms. "I knew you wanted them, babygirl. Ya'll enjoy, ya' hear," Ms. Channel said while she sauntered off and checked on her other tables.

Althea couldn't wait to dig into her mushrooms; she almost forgot Diamond was there until she felt him staring at her. "Oh, my bad. Did you want some? Sorry, they're my favorite and anytime me or Mother Rose come here, I never share."

"It's all good, babygirl. Enjoy," Diamond said with a smile that stretched across his entire face and made Althea melt.

Damn, I'm getting about as soft as these damn mushrooms. Focus, Thea, focus, she told herself. "So, what do you do? I haven't seen you at any school games, and I know you ain't from around here either."

"Oh, I do a little this and a little that," Diamond replied, now completely serious.

Althea noted the change in his demeanor, and she instantly knew that Diamond was a drug dealer. His hard edge stuck out through his nice smile no matter how charming he presented. Althea was quiet for a moment and ate. She wondered if he would be truthful about being a drug dealer. "So, you sell drugs?" she asked, her mouth full of mushrooms and head down.

"Naw, I have other people sell drugs for me. I'm the boss," Diamond said coolly. Althea looked up and their eyes met. In that moment, his whole face went dark. Althea could see the grime that he was capable of. They stared at one another, eyes locked for what seemed like an eternity. Diamond's eyes told Althea everything that she would ever need to know about his business. She decided right then, that would be the last time she ever asked him how he earned the wad of cash he so easily shared with her.

Ms. Channel approached the table with their food and could feel the cold exchange between Althea and Diamond. It made Ms. Channel so uncomfortable that she felt like she was intruding, so she cleared her throat when approaching their booth. She was glad she did because it broke the gaze they had transfixed on one another.

Diamond gave a nervous laugh. "Mmm...smells good." He looked up at Ms. Channel. She set both of their meals down, asked if there was anything else they needed, and quickly made her exit. Althea and Diamond both ate their food in silence while occasionally looking up at one another.

"I'm glad you invited me here, Althea. I had a good time just being here with you. It was dope," Diamond said while looking deeply into Althea's eyes. "I can't explain it, but..."

"What? What can't you explain?" Althea leaned in to ask.

"I have a connection with you, Althea, a strong one that I can't explain." Diamond looked up sheepishly at Althea, his eyes were wide with anticipation and worry. "I've been here a while and really haven't connected with anyone, but as soon as I saw you out on the floor, I knew I had to have you." Again, Diamond looked deep into Althea's eyes. Usually, she would respond with a sarcastic comeback, but she let Diamond's words linger in the air. She'd never had anyone be so serious with her. Only the local high school boys approached her—and old-ass men who knew she was underage but didn't care.

Diamond is different, she thought as she continued her meal. There was still a voice in the back of her mind saying, *don't trust him.* But for now, Althea pushed that voice to the furthest corner of her mind. She liked being adored and told how beautiful she was. She soaked up all the attention Diamond's eyes were silently giving her.

"Well, I can follow you home. Make sure you get home safe," Diamond said nonchalantly while adjusting his gold chain that had a small gold cross hanging from it.

Althea shot him a quick glance. *Oh, so that's his game. He wants to know where I live so he can come in and fuck! I knew he was too good to be true!* Althea thought. = She got up without a word and quickly made her way to her car. "Bye, Ms. Channel," she called over her shoulder.

"Althea, wait! Wait, Althea!" Diamond shouted after her. He hurried from the booth but realized he forgot to pay. He went back to their booth, threw a hundred-dollar bill on the table, and hurried after Althea. "Althea...wait! What I do?" Diamond was genuinely confused. He thought Althea and he made a real connection and they were both feeling each other. He didn't understand what went wrong in those few seconds.

Althea quickly unlocked her door, closed it, and was putting her key in the ignition when Diamond made it to her window. She looked at him panting with a confused look on his face. *Don't be confused now, dummy,* she thought. *Oh, he thought he had some young, dumb high school girl he could trick outta her panties by flashing a few hundred dollas? Well, he thought wrong.*

"Get away from my car Diamond," she yelled as she started her car. "You must think I'm stupid, huh? If you wanted to fuck, why didn't you just say so!" Althea was upset. How could she have let her guard down that fast? She took her.22 out of its hiding spot and politely placed it on her lap. She gave Diamond one last daring look as the confusion quickly flashed from his face and was replaced with stone when he saw the gun in Althea's lap. She quickly put her car in reverse, sped away, and didn't look back.

Ms. Channel came running out of the truck stop to see what the commotion was all about, but all she could see were Althea's fading taillights. "Hmph," Ms. Channel snorted and looked at Diamond. "Not a sweet little teen like you thought, huh? So, you still wanna place that to-go order for your granny, or was that a lie, too?" Ms. Channel asked with an attitude and walked back inside the truck stop.

Diamond drove home from the truck stop confused, replaying the entire evening between Althea and him on repeat. He simply could not understand what he did or said to make Althea flip the script on him so fast and storm out. He felt like he made a true connection with her, and she was feeling him, too. He usually had to dodge women in his hometown because they knew about his "business" and wanted a piece of the pie. That is the main reason he relocated to the sleepy midwestern town: to get away from the hustle and bustle of the fast city life. However, the city life never left him.

Chapter Thirteen

OUR LOVE

Diamond never thought about not being a gangsta or drug dealer; he only wanted to run his "business" with less rivalry and less police heat. He was well-known in his city for having the best dope on the block. He made sure his product was as pure as possible and even linked up with a direct connect from Mexico. He never wanted to be the face of his business, so when local law enforcement started rounding up people in his organization for selling drugs, he knew it was the perfect time to make a new start. He was barely out of his teenage years, but already he had seen enough strife, death, and degradation to considerably age him.

He was smart and streetwise, but this wasn't the life he always imagined for himself. Diamond yearned to be a family man and provider. He grew up without a father in the home and his grandmother raised him. His mother was in and out of his life due to her drinking, but Diamond didn't see it that way. He thought his mother was weak and that she chose drinking over him, and he hated her for it. He vowed to himself that he would never make his children feel unwanted or unloved. The only woman in his life who ever showed him love was his grandmother, Mary. She was sweet and kind but would slice you with her tongue if needed. She always knew the perfect time and place to deliver the message needed to pierce your heart and make you think.

Diamond loved his Grandma Mary with all his heart and soul. He knew that as long as she was alive, he had an angel here on earth watching out for him and protecting him. Grandma Mary, or Grandmother, as Diamond called her, moved from the harsh city with Diamond in part to look after him, but mainly because she sought a simpler life for herself as well in her later years.

Diamond pulled up to his house and sat for a while before he saw the curtain move. He knew it was his grandmother waiting for him to get out of the car. He sighed and reluctantly grabbed his to-go bag of food he had bought from the truck stop, knowing full well his grandmother already had breakfast waiting. When he opened the front door, he was greeted by the smell of peppered bacon and fresh baked biscuits, his favorite meal. He came inside the house, placed the to-go box in the refrigerator and gave his grandma a big squeeze.

"Why are girls so complicated?" Diamond breathed into his grandmother's neck while soaking up all her love.

His grandmother let out a low laugh and replied, "Now, that is a good question."

Diamond loved that his grandmother never pretended to have all the answers; she knew that a homecooked meal and a good hug could fix just about anything.

"Long night?" his grandmother asked without turning her head from her task of peeling potatoes. She always loved to work on lunch prep right after she finished cooking breakfast. His grandmother loved to cook!

"Yeah, I had a long night. I met a girl, and just when I thought things were going good, she ran out on me."

"Well, what did you say or do right before she ran out?"

"I asked her if I could follow her home to make sure she got there safely," Diamond replied while he sat heavily in one of the two kitchen chairs.

"Well, baby, everybody ain't like you. Maybe that was too forward of you to ask to come to her house. Did you ever think about that?"

Silence filled the kitchen as Diamond replayed the night and how fast things had turned for the worst. He also was shocked that Althea pulled out a gun, although she didn't point it at him; she must've really felt like she was going to be hurt.

"Uuuugh," Diamond let out a sigh and placed his hands on his face and leaned back in the kitchen chair. "I don't know," he muttered, more to himself than to his grandmother. "I'm gonna get some rest, gotta be up in a few anyways. I'll eat then."

Diamond felt like weights were dragging him down, and he realized how exhausted he was and headed to his room. His grandmother didn't even turn her head to look after him, but she sheepishly smiled because she was happy that her baby was interested in a girl long enough to take notice of her. She knew he was smitten.

Diamond went to sleep with thoughts of Althea in his head. He tossed and turned, worrying about the last impression she had and how he was going to turn it around. He went about his week as usual, making deals, moving product, and lying low in the shadows. All the while Althea was on his mind.

Months passed by without any major incidents in the drug game, which was rare. Diamond decided to stop by the gas station to grab a quick drink before checking on all his spots. As he pulled into the gas station, he surveyed the parking lot out of habit because he never knew who was watching and waiting for him to slip and become the prey. He couldn't believe it! Althea was pumping gas. A smile quickly engulfed his whole being. If he was honest with himself, he had been quietly searching for Althea since the day she ran off from the truck stop. He knew he had to play it cool. He knew she wasn't like any regular chick and that's what turned him on. He sat and watched her through his rearview mirror while he noted her demeanor had somewhat changed since the last time he saw her. Althea's shoulders were hunched, and she wore a track suit with an older pair of Jordan's. Her hair was in a messy bun. He suddenly had the urge to go to her, make whatever was bothering her go away. He quickly turned off the engine and made his way to the opposite side of Althea's pump.

"So how much you putting in? You need some help with that?" Diamond smiled on the other side of the pump, imagining Althea recognizing his voice and smiling back. But instead, he heard Althea vigorously hanging up the gas pump. Diamond moved from around the pump to stand in front of Althea's car, now facing her.

Althea took one glance at Diamond and opened her front door to climb inside. "Hold up, now, wait!" Diamond pleaded.

He took one giant step and grabbed Althea's door before she could close it. "Look, I think we got off on the wrong foot, Althea. I owe you an apology," Diamond stammered. He didn't know how much time he had or when he would run into Althea again, so he knew he had to be quick. "Look, no disrespect, but I just wanna get to know you." He looked Althea deep in her eyes and saw hurt.

Diamond moved from the other side of the door and knelt in front of Althea. "What's wrong? You can tell me...what is it?"

Diamond's eyes pleaded with Althea for her to tell the truth. And at that moment, Diamond was just what Althea needed: a protector. Althea looked in Diamond's eyes and tears began to fall.

"Hold on, hold on, babygirl, what's all this?" Diamond said sweetly and embraced Althea. When he did, Althea began to shake and sob in

Diamond's arms. "What's wrong, Althea, somebody hurt you? You know I got people for that...what's wrong?"

Althea wiggled out of Diamond's embrace. "It's just Mother Rose. Ummm...I mean my mom, she's in jail and I don't know when she gettin' out. And the small bit of money I had saved is almost gone, my best friend ain't my best friend anymore, and I ain't got nobody else." Althea sniffed and silently cried.

"Damn," Diamond replied and hugged Althea again. "I got you now, you ain't gotta worry. You hear me? I got you. C'mon, let's get outta here, snakes is watching. Follow me to the park so we can talk."

Althea nodded in agreement, gathered herself, and drove to the nearest park. Althea got out of the car and automatically walked to a picnic table and sat on top of it, resting her feet on the bench. Diamond was right behind her. By the time Althea made it to the park, she had already made her mind up that Diamond would be her man and they would be together. The pair sat talking until the sun went down.

"Look, get yo' stuff, you can't stay in that house by yourself, especially with these snake ass niggas knowing Mother Rose is gone. They gonna try you. You can stay with me and my grandmother."

Althea raised her brow. "Stay with you and your grandmother? Boy, what I look like?"

"Shit, you look like my woman. And I want you with me," Diamond said with authority. He reached out and grabbed Althea's face and kissed her hard with passion that had built up for months and finally found release. "Is you wit' it?" Diamond asked Althea between tongue kisses. Althea breathlessly nodded in agreement.

The two spent every waking moment they could together. The only time they were apart was when Diamond had to make business runs and Althea had to go to school. Summer was almost here, and

Althea couldn't wait because then she would have even more time to spend with Diamond. She really liked living with Diamond and his grandmother even though Althea got the feeling his grandmother only tolerated her out of love for her grandson. A few months passed by with the two living together, eating, making love, going to the movies, tearing the mall down, and every other thing young lovers do.

Althea started showing up to school in outfits more fly than the ones Mother Rose had bought her. She also drove a new car every couple of weeks, and of course, she made a scene when she pulled into the school parking lot, bumping the latest song on her Alpine stereo. She loved seeing the girls roll their eyes and the guys fawn over her interchangeable rides. She had it all: a man who loved and adored her, and now she found out she had a baby on the way. She was super excited because she would be able to go through the end of her pregnancy in the summertime and be able to come back to school with no one being the wiser.

But news of Althea's pregnancy quickly spread through the school because she was, in fact, one of the most popular girls. One of her classmates noticed her growing belly in gym while Althea was changing and alerted the whole school. But she didn't care who knew she was pregnant because nothing could awaken her from her hood fairytale. She had everything she wanted: a fine man who dicked her down on a regular basis and loved her, a stable home environment where she was no longer being left alone like Mother Rose had done, and she her own family growing inside her. Althea couldn't have known what was coming next.

❋❋❋❋

Shots rang out, guided by fingers of jealousy and piercing the air with uncertainty. Diamond lay in a pool of his own blood. Killed by yellow-eyed enemies, leaving behind Althea and little Golden. The trio had four years, four good years of pure joy and happiness. All that love, all that hope...gone with a few bullets and sprays of blood.

Diamond's killers couldn't have known what their actions put into motion. There was no way of them knowing the dark path Althea would travel for the rest of her life, mourning the purest of loves she'd ever felt. The killers couldn't have known the hole they left in little Golden's life. A life without a father to guide her. A life without a protector, without someone to walk her down the aisle. How could they have known that the way those bullets shredded Diamond's body would also shred the futures of his family and hold them in perpetual grief? How were they to know that Althea and Golden would never again trust any good thing that came their way, knowing how easily life could snuff out happiness and steal it forever? There was no way they could know what their bullets set in motion...there was no way they could've known.

Chapter Fourteen

DIRTY HANDS

After Golden's blowup with Althea, she thought it a perfect time to visit Tatiana. Tatiana had wanted Golden to visit her in Vegas for months, but Golden always declined. Golden felt like this was as good a time as any to visit Tatiana. "Hey girl, I'm thinking about coming your way, is it still cool?

"Hell yeah, girl!" Tatiana screamed over the phone. "I can't wait to see you when you get here. I'm gonna tell my man that you're coming. I already told you, you don't have to worry about nothing when you come here. I'm so excited my girl is coming to town!"

Tatiana was talking a mile a minute and Golden could barely keep up. All she knew was that she was welcome and that's all she needed. Golden hung up her cell and headed straight for the airport, bags in tow.

*Damn...*she thought. *What will I do with my car while I'm in Vegas?* There was only one person she trusted...Marquez.

"Hey, do you mind if I park my car at your garage for a few days? I just need to get away from my momma. We got into it, and I just need a few days to clear my head," Golden asked Marquez. She knew he would never refuse her requests, no matter how much he didn't agree or understand her thought process.

"Sure, baby, if that's what you need. Where you gonna go? You leaving town? When you coming back?" Marquez pelted Golden with questions and didn't even wait for an answer before he asked the next one. He didn't like seeing Golden upset and he definitely didn't like her dancing at the club. He could see her changing right before his eyes the past couple of months. So, naturally, he was worried about her well-being.

Golden sighed. "Ugh...I'm just going to visit my girl Tatiana in Vegas for a few days to clear my head. I can't live with my momma no more!" She looked him in the eye, and he saw how tired she was. Golden's beautiful green eyes had more of a gray cast to them. And it was the first time Marquez noticed bags under Golden's eyes. So, he decided to lay off and end his tirade of questions.

"Okay, just a few days, right? Then you'll be back?" Marquez's eyes pleaded with Golden's for an answer he could believe. But he had a funny feeling in his gut that it would be a very long time before he saw Golden's beautiful face.

Golden made her travel arrangements and booked a one-way flight to Vegas for the next morning. She decided she would camp out at the airport until the morning when her flight was scheduled to leave. She didn't have a clue when she was coming back or if she ever wanted to. She just knew that she needed to put space between her and her mom and the day-to-day grind of the V. She decided to get a large storage unit to store her car and the few clothes she'd taken from her house. She didn't even want to have to deal with Marquez's probing questions about when she was coming back home. While she was sitting at the airport, waiting for her flight, Golden began to think about how she moved so fast, she forgot to say goodbye to her grandmother. *Damn,* she thought.

"Hey, Grandma," Golden said weakly when her grandmother answered the phone. Now she felt a pang of guilt as she thought about leaving her aging grandmother alone with Althea without saying goodbye.

"Hey baby, how you doing?" Golden's grandmother took an audible loud breath as she adjusted herself, sitting up in bed to talk to Golden. "Ya' momma told me you and her got into it the other day. Now, I don't even wanna get into it because I already know it was behind some mess! I just wanna know if you okay and when you coming home?" Golden's grandmother sat patiently on the phone waiting for Golden to give her an answer.

"Grandma...I really don't know. I just need a minute to clear my head, ya' know? So much stuff has been going on and things moving so fast, I haven't had time to think."

"Mmmm-hmmm, I get that," her grandmother softly replied.

"I'm on my way to Vegas for a few days to chill with one of my friend-girls. I'll be back soon. I left you some money in the green tin behind your mirror in your room. That should be enough to hold you until I get back."

The phone was silent for so long that Golden said, "Hello...Grandmother? Did you hear what I said about me going to Vegas and the money?" Still no answer. "Hello...Grandmother?"

Golden's grandmother let out a long sigh. "Well, baby, I knew this day would come when you would spread your wings and fly away. You were always my little Golden butterfly, just ready to soar." More silence. "Just don't forget who you are baby, never forget who you are."

"Yes, ma'am," Golden replied solemnly.

"Well, let me get up and make these grits cuz they ain't gonna make themselves. You know ya momma gonna need something to coat that stomach after all that licka."

"Love you, Grandmother. I'm gonna call you when I get there."

"Okay, baby. Love you too."

Golden hung up the phone with an aching in her heart, missing her grandmother. She felt guilty knowing she left her grandmother at home to take care of her dysfunctional mother. Golden felt tears welling up in the corners of her eyes and shook it off. She told herself that it was her life and her time to live. She could no longer live for her grandmother or mother, or anyone else for that matter.

Golden got her bags from the baggage claim and realized she didn't make any plans to be picked up from the airport. Furthermore, she didn't even know Tatiana's address. All Golden knew was that she needed to get away and Vegas sounded like a good option. Golden decided she would call Tatiana as soon as she got to the airport exit; she just wanted to breathe the fresh Vegas air.

"Hey, girl! I'm in your city!" Golden screamed to Tatiana when she answered the phone. I'm getting my bags from the baggage claim, but I just remembered I forgot to ask your address, girl, my nerves just so bad!"

"It's all good, boo. I sent a car for you. He should be there at the edge of baggage claim waiting for you. I'm so excited you finally decided to come. I can't wait to see you!" Tatiana screamed so loudly, Golden had to inch her phone away from her ear. "The driver will bring you to the house. I can't wait to see you." Tatiana didn't even say goodbye before hanging up.

Golden raised a brow and smiled. She knew that Tatiana never said goodbye. She once told Golden that she grew up in foster care and never got used to saying goodbye to people. Saying goodbye meant she would be on her way to a new home, the unknown waiting on the other side, so she decided she would never say goodbye again.

Golden found her way to baggage claim and looked toward the exit. Sure enough, she saw a driver holding a sign with her name on it. Golden walked up to the clean-cut driver and gave him an awkward smile. The driver simply nodded, grabbed her luggage, and headed through the automatic doors of the airport exit. The driver briskly walked to an all-black SUV with deeply tinted windows. The driver opened the door for Golden and promptly closed the door, opened the SUV hatch, and placed Golden's bag inside. The driver climbed into the driver's seat and said, "We have about a twenty-minute drive." Then, he looked straight ahead and rolled up the privacy glass. Golden was initially offended at the abruptness of the driver, but then she sunk into the soft leather seats and was grateful for the quiet moment. Golden felt like she had been going a hundred miles an hour since she left home and boarded her flight.

Golden was awakened by the rocking of the SUV. She didn't even realize when she fell asleep or how long she had been asleep. As she looked out the window, Golden saw only a long driveway with walled brick on either side. She felt gravity pull her back to her seat as she struggled to sit forward, so she knew they were driving at an incline. The driveway seemed to go on forever. The walls were so high that all Golden could see was the sky. She didn't know if she was in a neighborhood or the desert. The SUV came to a stop in front of a large, white metal gate opening to the right. The SUV slowly proceeded forward, and a huge two-story modern home built on a hillside came into view. Golden audibly gasped because the view of the house was breathtaking. It was something straight out of a movie. The house looked like a white outline covered in glass. Golden's thoughts started to race because she thought she had gotten into the wrong SUV. There was no way this could be Tatiana's house. She was so tired when she arrived at the airport, she stopped questioning her surroundings because it took too much energy to be aware and she was exhausted. She questioned herself. *Did the driver really hold a sign that had her name on it at the airport?* Golden didn't even ask for any credentials; she just got into the SUV. Now she felt so stupid...like a lamb being led to the slaughter.

The SUV slowed to a stop on the paved circle drive. The driver quickly hopped out and retrieved Golden's bags from the car and carried them to the large, dark-stained wooden door. Just as Golden was about to ask the driver a question, the front door opened to a small woman dressed in a modern maid's uniform. She opened the door widely and motioned for Golden to come inside. Golden hesitantly stepped inside the foyer of this beautiful home. She could not help but notice everything in the home was white and accented in black. The floors were a white marble that nearly reflected her face. Golden stood in the doorway awkwardly for so long, the maid had to motion her to come inside with a friendly smile. "Hello, Miss Golden. Can I get you anything to drink? I know you've had a long trip," the maid asked Golden in a soft tone, covered in a heavy accent.

"No...no...I'm fine," Golden stammered. Golden turned her head and noticed the driver leave as quickly as he came. *Dang, there goes my escape,* Golden thought

Just then, Golden heard the clacking of heels faintly coming from the left side of the house. Golden looked in the direction of the approaching footsteps as they grew louder. The maid gave a quick nod and retreated to an unknown corner of the house with Golden's suitcase in tow. Golden felt her anxiety rise. *Why did she just leave? Whose house am I in? Oh, Lawd, I'm about to die!* Golden's thoughts were racing illogically.

"Ahhhhhhh!" Tatiana screamed as she came into view from around the corner from the left of the kitchen. "You made it, bitch!" Tatiana quickened her step and tiptoed her way over to Golden with her arms outstretched. Golden stood there frozen. Her mind and her eyes were not making the connection between her stripper friend and the woman she saw before her with outstretched hands. Tatiana wore a dark green and black swimsuit in giraffe print with gold bangles, gold necklace, and a sheer green cover up over her swimsuit that glided with her when she walked. Golden stood still like a statue while Tatiana crashed into her with a long embrace.

Tatiana didn't feel Golden hug her back and quickly stepped back, still holding onto Golden's shoulders. "Hey. Boo, what's wrong? You okay? I know you had a long flight. Let's get you settled."

Tatiana gave Golden's shoulders a firm squeeze and reached down to grasp her hand firmly. Tatiana gave Golden's hand a quick jerk as if to move Golden from the spot she was stuck in. Golden wriggled her hand free.

"What is this, T?" Golden stopped walking and folded her arms.

"What is what?" Tatiana asked coyly. She knew exactly what Golden was asking: How did a girl like her end up in a mansion like this?

"You know what the fuck I mean, T! What is this? What the fuck are we doing here? You got me down here on some bullshit?" Golden's voice deepened with seriousness. She knew Tatiana always had a scheme going, but she never thought she would involve her in one of them.

"Girl, stop trippn'. I live here, Golden. Well, I live here with my man. This is his house." Tatiana grabbed Golden's arm again, trying to ease her further into the house.

"If I knew you was on some bullshit, T, I never woulda come. I been going through a lot and needed a break, but I ain't about to be mixed up in some mess. So, you tell me right now, what the fuck is going on before I take another step!" Golden demanded while folding her arms and pursing her lips. She glowered at Tatiana, waiting for an explanation.

"Ugh! Okay…damn, you ain't no fun! Well, can we at least sit by the pool and talk?" Tatiana looked sincere and Golden never could find a way to tell her no, even from the moment they met.

"Fine, bitch, as long as we can have a drink by the pool." Golden smiled and gave in to Tatiana. They walked hand-in-hand to the pool. As Golden traveled through the house she looked up at a chandelier that had so many crystals on it, she couldn't help to think how much it must have cost. She was so enamored by the chandelier she tripped over the first step leading up to the kitchen and living area. Golden forgot she saw these four or five steps when she initially entered the mansion. She noted the sky-to-ceiling windows that showcased the view to the backyard—if it could even be called that. Golden's jaw dropped as she looked at Tatiana in wonder. Tatiana sheepishly smiled. She knew what Golden was thinking because she had the same reaction when she saw this magnificent view for the first time. The only difference was, she acted like she was unimpressed, like she saw these types of homes all the time. This thought was partly true; Tatiana had seen herself in a mansion like this one day, but only in her wildest dreams.

Tatiana opened the retractable, all-glass wall with the touch of a button on a remote and a swoop of hot air rushed inside the home. There was a conveniently place bar under a large awning attached to the house that the two women gravitated toward. Tatiana went to work behind the bar. "So, what you wanna know?"

"First of all, whose house is this and do they know you're here?" Golden asked as she leaned in with a smirk.

"This is my man's house. I met him at one of the clubs I do rounds at, and we just clicked. You know, men with power who love a good rags-to-riches story? You know the type, girl. always tryna save a hoe! They always tell you they really don't go to strip clubs, and they just got out of a serious relationship or just got divorced. Lucky for me, my man was recently divorced and a little lovesick puppy. So, I put this mouth and pussy on him, and the rest is history," Tatiana said while sliding Golden her glass and raising it in a toast.

"Well, I'm not mad at you, bitch. See, I could get used to this," Golden said and looked out toward the infinity pool that seemed to melt into the arid Nevada mountains.

"So, what happened with you and your mom?"

Golden kept looking into the horizon as if she didn't hear Tatiana's question. She sighed. "I really don't wanna talk about it," Golden replied. She turned around on the barstool to face Tatiana. "Actually, I'm kind of tired. I didn't know how tired I was from all that travel until right now."

"It's all good, boo. Go get some rest. Oh! My man wanted to host a welcome party for you tonight." Tatiana let a sly smile crawl across her lips.

Golden looked back and rolled her eyes and head. "Ugh...a party? Yeah, I'm definitely gonna need a nap."

Golden had so many questions about who Tatiana's man was and why he wanted to throw her a party, but at that very moment, her brain was too exhausted to pick apart Tatiana's mastermind.

Tatiana showed Golden to her room where the housekeeper had already unpacked her clothing and put away her things in the closet and dresser drawers. Golden was thankful that she didn't have to be burdened with unpacking. She was so exhausted that she didn't even shower. Golden pulled off her shoes, socks, and clothes. She pulled back the plush blankets and slid inside the cool covers in only her bra and panties; she was in a deep sleep before she realized.

Golden was awakened by the muffled sounds of laughing voices and soft jazz music playing in the distance. She strained her ears while her eyes were still closed to decipher how many voices she heard, but she quickly gave up. Golden forgot where she was for a split-second. Then she remembered she was at Tatiana's house and vaguely remembered her mentioning a party in her honor. Golden slowly sat up in bed and grabbed her phone from the side table. *Damn…it's dead,* she thought. She forgot to charge her cell before she went to sleep. She sighed guiltily because she knew her grandma must be worried sick about her. Golden got up from the bed and looked around the room to determine where the housekeeper may have put her charger. Luckily for Golden, she didn't have to look too far; her charger was on the opposite side table next to her bed. She quickly grabbed the charger to plug in her phone. She heard laughing voices again. Golden got up to peek out of her bedroom window and noticed that it was already dark outside. *Geez, how long was I asleep?"* she thought.

She noticed just beyond the shrubs of the house were beautiful lanterns everywhere emitting a soft glow throughout the backyard. Golden turned away from the window and noticed an emerald green dress laying neatly in the corner of the sitting area. Below the dress was a sexy pair of strappy heels with stones on the toe and straps that wrapped around the ankle. A small smile creeped over Golden's face because she knew this was Tatiana's doing. She had impeccable taste in clothing, so Golden knew the dress would snugly fit her curves and push her breasts to the high heavens. As Golden walked closer to the dress, she noticed a small note folded on top: *Wear this tonight, T.*

Golden skipped into the bathroom to take a shower and get dressed. The apprehension she once felt being in this huge mansion quickly dissipated once she found the handwritten note from her friend.

Deciding not to let the beautiful rainfall shower go to waste, Golden gathered her shower items. Golden thought that a high sleek ponytail would be perfect for the dress Tatiana chose. Golden always traveled with hair options: wigs, packs of loose hair, and phony ponies. She quickly showered and washed her hair. She noticed she had forgotten to get a wax prior to leaving home due to her frame of mind in the aftermath of her argument with her mother. *Oh well, the stubble isn't noticeable on my dark skin. Plus it's already dark outside. It's not like I'm giving lap dances,* Golden thought.

Golden decided on a bronze goddess theme for the party. She used a bronze and silver metallic eye shadow that she blended to perfection, topped her eyes with a wispy pair of lashes, and completed with green, winged liner. She admired how her green liner intensified the hue of her green eyes. Then she used a metallic green eye shadow underneath her lower lid to further accentuate her eye color. She added her favorite bronze highlighter that made her cheekbones pop in all the desirable ways. She added a strong brow and nude matte lip to complete her look. She gathered her damp hair into a high bun and chose to wear a braided bun instead of a sleek ponytail. She chose to wear her two-carat diamond earrings with rose gold backing. She completed her look with her favorite body oil and perfume. Golden slipped into her dressed and heels and followed the laughter and music.

Golden was pleasantly surprised by how beautiful the backyard looked in the moonlight combined with the soft, yellow lighting of the lanterns strung about. As soon as she walked onto the back patio, she was greeted with a glass of champaign from a server, which Golden gladly took. She eagerly scanned the room for Tatiana. Tatiana was standing at a table at the far side of the infinity pool. She appeared to be laughing and entertaining her guests. Golden noted a gentleman standing next to her with his arm wrapped loosely around Tatiana's small waist. Tatiana wore a white, formfitting dress with a plunging neckline. The man standing next to her was clearly significantly older than Tatiana: his smile revealed deep-set wrinkles around his eyes. Golden surmised the man was not prematurely gray but was Tatiana's sugar daddy. Golden sipped her champagne and continued to assess Tatiana and her man. The stranger wore white dress pants topped with a powder blue dinner jacket and white leather loafers. He had a large, gold- and diamond-encrusted pinky ring that glistened by lantern light. Golden stood staring at the strange man, wondering who he was and how Tatiana snagged him. The small crowd that was gathered around Tatiana followed her toward Golden where she stood in the shadows, secretly assessing them. Their stares were so obvious that Tatiana motioned to Golden while mouthing the words "come here." Tatiana broke from the crowd, almost knocking over the man standing next to her with her long trundles of hair.

Tatiana stifled a satisfied grin when she saw Golden. She knew Golden was a baddie, and she also knew that Golden had a look that only one in a million women had: a dark-skinned girl with green eyes, big titties, and a fat ass! Tatiana could damned near hear Golden's heels hit the concrete surrounding the pool, even over the loud DJ, because all conversations stilled for a moment and all eyes were on her. As she got closer and they locked eyes, Golden knew what Tatiana was up. *We gonna take these damn squares for every penny they got.*

Golden walked up to Tatiana and gave her a hug around her waist, and the two were instantly in sync, scanning the room for lusting eyes. "I want to make a toast to my beautiful friend Layla," Tatiana said as she raised her champagne glass. She looked at Golden with the widest smile and Golden returned the favor, smiling with her eyes and lifting her glass.

"To Layla," the guests said in unison while the tinkling of glasses added a certain sweetness to the night air. Golden now understood why Tatiana was so pressed to have Golden come to Vegas. She always spoke of the men, money, and extravagant lifestyle that Vegas provided. When Tatiana grew tired of one cash cow, she moved on to the next. Golden smiled sweetly at the onlookers but could not fight a feeling of resentment toward Tatiana. She was in no place mentally to be a man's fantasy or hustle him out of his money. She really needed a friend and a place to gather her thoughts and plan the next step of her life. *That won't happen tonight,"* she thought as she sipped her champagne.

The next morning Golden awoke with a slight hangover from the champagne and lack of food from the previous night. She decided to put on her bathing suit and sit by the pool to recover in peace. The early morning sun gently warmed her cool skin. She relaxed and sunk into her recliner with her arm covering her forehead to shield it from the sun's rays. She drifted off a bit as her breathing turned from shallow to deep, relaxing breaths. She thought about her grandmother and how she needed to call her when she got back to her room to let her know she made it safely to Vegas.

The clicking sound of heels on concrete became louder as Golden opened her eyes halfway in anticipation. "Hey beautiful, good morning," Tatiana's voice chimed. Golden's eyes opened and had to adjust to the sunlight. She saw Tatiana's silhouette approaching as her eyes adjusted. Tatiana had on a white bathing suit with a plunging neckline and an off the shoulder, sheer coverup. Golden couldn't see Tatiana's face because it was covered by a large sunhat that left only the ends of her hair visible. "I brought you water."

Golden's throat tightened at the thought of water. She was probably already dehydrated and was unable to tell how long she had been sunbathing.

"Girl, are you crazy? You do not sit out in this Vegas heat without a sunhat or shade! You are not in the Midwest anymore, honey," Tatiana teased as she sat down and handed Golden one of the waters she carried.

Golden greedily gulped down the water and sat in silence waiting for Tatiana to make the first move. She didn't want to ask her any questions about last night or why she used an alias for Golden. She wanted to know her angle and didn't want to play coy about it; she was too exhausted for games.

The two sat for a while before Tatiana broke the silence. "So, last night was fun, right?" Tatiana asked brightly.

Golden shielded her eyes to look directly at Tatiana, "Uhn huh." Golden remained silent. She knew that Tatiana couldn't wait to reveal her masterplan she was working on, so she remained silent until Tatiana couldn't take it anymore.

"So how has business been? You like working at the clubs?" Tatiana was fishing.

Where was this line of questioning headed? Golden thought. She decided to nod in agreement. She knew her friend couldn't stand to drag things out, so Golden decided to have some fun and torture Tatiana a bit.

"So, have you made exclusive headlining deals like how I taught you?"

Again, Golden nodded but did not make eye contact with Tatiana this time. "And how's home life going? Your mom and grandmother good?"

Golden nodded.

"So have you ever thought about escorting?"

"Bitch, what?" Golden sat up and swiftly turned to face Tatiana full-on in one move. "Escort? Tati, what in the hell you talkn' 'bout? Hell naw! Have you?" Golden asked half-jokingly and reclined back in her pool chair.

"Welllll...that's what I kinda wanted to talk to you about," Tatiana uncomfortably shifted in her seat.

Golden leaned in, looking under Tatiana's hat so she could see her eyes, realizing her friend was serious.

"I mean, damn, Golden, how you think I get all these clothes, jewels, cars, and money?"

Golden's mouth was open in shock. "Wait, wait, wait. I'm confused. I've seen all the money you make at the club and that ain't no small amount of cash."

"And it ain't no small amount of cash that keeps me looking this good either. I gotta pay for the upkeep of my body, facials, body sculpting, lip injections, weaves, costumes, makeup, high rise living. All that shit adds up Golden. And don't sit up here and act like you ain't fucked no nigga for a bag before." Tatiana started to raise her voice.

Golden could sense her friend feeling judged, "I just didn't think you got down like that, that's all Tati."

The two sat silent for another few moments. "Well, it's not like I'm fucking all these guys. Most times I just go out with these high rollers and be their eye candy when they come into town, you know make 'em feel like they got a big dick."

Golden remained silent. She was still trying to process what her friend just divulged. She always thought Tatiana was a boss and would never let a man objectify her and use her body. She really admired Tati for showing her the game without having to give hand jobs and blow jobs in VIP like some of the other girls in the club. She was silently going over all the rules Tatiana ever told her about trading money for sex when her thoughts were interrupted.

"Look, I thought you could handle it. I didn't know you were gonna act like such a baby about it." Tatiana flipped her hair off her shoulders and drank some of her water. "Look Golden, I ain't gonna bullshit you. I really thought you had a clue about what I was doing here, so when you said you were coming out here, I thought that was you saying you were ready to get down."

Both women remained silent for a while.

"C'mon girl, let's get you outta this sun," Tatiana said after a while.

Golden continued to sit motionless, still processing.

Tatiana reached out, grabbing Golden's hand. "I'm sorry, girl, for real. I wasn't trying to blindside you. For real, I love you like a sister...forgive me?" Tatiana gave a huge smile. Golden could never stay mad at her too long.

Golden rolled her eyes. "Whatever, hoe. Let's get outta this sun before I get any damn darker." They both laughed.

From the outside, Tatiana and Golden looked like sweet, young girls who may do a little blow and have free sex, but to think that would be like believing a lion cub stays small and adorable. These two women were born hustlers and had dreams of their own. Getting their hands dirty was just a part of their hustle.

Chapter Fifteen

RENT-A-GIRL

Golden picked up her cell phone, remembering to call her grandmother. She wanted to let her know she was okay and was going to be home soon. Golden missed her already but needed this time to clear her head and think about her next move. She really liked what Vegas had to offer, the little she'd seen of it.

"Hello," Golden's grandmother answered in a soft tone.

"Hey, Grandma, it's me Golden, I was just calling to check on you and let you know I made it to Vegas safely." Golden nestled her phone in the crook of her neck to wash her hands, then she decided to wash her face, too, since it looked a little oily from being in the sun. She always double-cleansed her face to ensure her makeup would be flawless by working with an already clean canvas. "Hey, Grandma, can you hear me?

"Yes, baby, I can hear you," Grandmother said weakly.

Golden put her phone on speaker and continued her cleansing routine. "So, I was just calling to say hi and I'll probably be home sometime next week. I really like it out here. You know I'm out here with Tati. She said she's gonna show me the Vegas strip tonight so that should be fun, you know how Tati likes to do things big."

Her grandmother let out a small laugh because she did know how extravagant Tatiana could be; she realized that the first time she met her. Golden reached across the large marble countertop for her face towel with one eye halfway open, avoiding getting leftover cleanser and water in her eyes.

"Oh, shit!" Golden accidently pushed her phone into the running water. She quickly reached her hand in the sink to retrieve her phone. "Hello...hello, Grandmother, can you hear me? Dang it!" Her screen went dark immediately. She already had cracks in her screen and had plans to buy another phone soon, so now it was a must. *Oh well, I needed a new phone anyway,* Golden thought. She planned on getting a new phone in the morning so she could finish her conversation with her grandmother. She knew her grandmother was probably confused by the abrupt ending of their conversation since they always ended in "I love you." For now, Golden was satisfied that she heard her grandmother's voice and had reassured her she would be home next week.

She excitedly finished getting dressed. Golden was curious to know what Tatiana planned for this evening's festivities. Earlier in the afternoon, Tatiana loaned Golden a slinky, silver mesh minidress that moved every time she moved. Golden's beautiful five-ten frame was exquisitely outlined by her dress. Golden decided to wear a pair of black, high-waisted, lace thongs and let "the girls" be free. She stared at herself in the mirror and admired how the cool, metallic mesh of her dress made her nipples slightly erect, creating a sensual look for the night and perfect for Vegas. Plus, she thought it was too hot for unnecessary clothing. She decided on a long sleek, jet-black wig with a blunt-cut bang covering her eyebrows. Her lips were a glossy nude color in combination with a matte finish aloe-colored smokey eye to complement her natural eye color.

"Damn, girl!" Tatiana exclaimed when Golden swayed into the foyer of the house. "I should've saved that dress for myself," Tatiana lamented. Tatiana was dressed in a neon yellow bodycon dress with a v-cut bodice, and the back was entirely open except for fine threading that intricately laced the back of her dress. Tatiana's full back tattoo of heaven and hell was visible. Golden loved Tatiana's back tattoo and how it came to life as Tatiana moved and swayed her body. That was one of the first things Golden took note of when she saw Tatiana dance for the first time. She never saw a woman who was completely in tune with her body, and Golden admired how she effortlessly animated her back tattoo with the slightest shift in fluid movement.

"You ladies look beautiful," she heard a voice say from the corner. It was Tatiana's boyfriend, benefactor, sugar daddy, or all the above. Golden still wasn't sure which, and she didn't plan on asking Tatiana to define the silver fox's relationship because she was still reeling from Tatiana's escort confession earlier that day. She just wanted to enjoy her friend and Vegas, of course! "Here, baby." The silver fox smoothly walked up to Tatiana and handed her a credit card and full money clip. "You two beautiful ladies have fun."

Tatiana tilted her head and slowly walked over to the silver fox. "Thank you, Daddy." She pressed her body against his, kissed him sweetly on the cheek, and pulled back. The silver fox closed his eyes, leaning forward and angling Tatiana's chin up to meet his lips, and sunk his grasp into the small of her back, guiding her body back in slowly and pressing himself upon her. They engaged in an innocent kiss that made Golden blush as she looked away. Tatiana began to stroke the outside of the silver fox's pants, and she plucked the credit card and money out of his hand, stepping back. "See you in a bit, babe. Don't wait up," she said as she bit her bottom lip. She then turned on her heels, locking eyes with Golden and motioning with her eyes toward the door. Golden followed suit and gave a weak, "Thank you," toward the silver fox's direction, quickly following Tatiana to the tinted SUV awaiting them.

The lights of the Las Vegas strip in the distance reflected in the tinted window of the SUV. A driver quickly hopped out of the driver's seat to open the back door. Golden allowed Tatiana to catch up with her so she could enter the SUV first. After Tatiana slid into the SUV, Golden peeked inside and saw a handsome stranger, and her mouth flew open as she let out a small gasp. She couldn't believe that Tatiana was comfortable meeting another man at her benefactor's door. As the driver closed the door on Golden, she glanced out the window as the SUV pulled off and saw the silver fox standing on the steps, watching them as they left. *So, he's okay with this?* Golden questioned in her head. She stared out of the window, trying to put together the pieces, but to no avail; she couldn't figure out why or how a man Tatiana was living with and apparently having sex with would allow her to go out with another man.

Then Golden realized that the silver fox must be a mash-up between a pimp, benefactor, or escort owner. Either way, she figured this arrangement had to be lucrative for Tatiana to stay. Golden continued to look out of her window in silence as Tatiana and the stranger made small talk. She tried to put aside the feeling of uneasiness growing inside her, deciding to focus on having a good time and enjoying herself in Vegas. *That's what I'll focus on,* she resigned to herself. She wasn't going to think about Tatiana's life as an escort, stripper, or possible high-end prostitute. She was determined to focus on getting wasted for free and forgetting her problems back home. She thought about how she always wanted to go to a Vegas show and couldn't believe she was on her way in a $12,000-dress, $4,000-bag, and $2,000-shoes, all gifted to her by Tatiana. She felt, looked, and smelled expensive, and she settled on enjoying every moment.

Tatiana's voice broke through Golden's inner monologue by introducing her to the handsome stranger, yet again, using another alias. As they drove along, Golden could see the bright lights of the Vegas strip in the distance. "First night in Vegas?" Tatiana's handsome stranger asked Golden in a thick accent she could not place.

Golden didn't answer him directly but smiled coyly at the handsome stranger. She knew men like that really didn't care about a woman's opinion or story; they only wanted small talk and sex. Golden gave him just that as they clanked champaign flutes in one toast after another. Golden was grateful for the free-flowing champagne that made her forget all the questions swirling in her head about Tatiana, the silver fox, and the handsome stranger. In between forced high-pitched laughs and champagne toasts, Golden thought about her grandmother and felt a heartache that made her visibly shift in her seat because their conversation ended so abruptly.

"What's wrong?" Tatiana asked Golden with genuine concern in her voice, noticing the shift in energy.

"Oh! I accidently dropped my phone in some water before we left," Golden immediately blurted.

"That's an easy fix," the stranger replied.

Golden smiled and tilted her head and condescendingly nodded and smirked in agreement at the stranger. *Who asked him?* she thought. Golden couldn't wait to get to a bar so she could order a real drink; all the champagne was making her light-headed and unusually emotional. She never liked to drink champagne at Club V either because she quickly learned the effects champagne had on her, which only slowed her money flow. She had so many questions and she knew none of them would be answered that night. So, Golden decided to enjoy the free entertainment and embrace where the night would lead. *Afterall, I am in Vegas,* she thought with a sly smile.

They finally made it to the Vegas strip and Golden loved seeing the lights and people milling about on the streets. There were so many signs and things to see that she felt her senses overload. She suddenly felt claustrophobic and rolled the window down halfway. Golden inhaled deeply and let the neon lights wash over her. She loved the way the crisp, Vegas night air felt after a long, hot day.

The SUV pulled in front of a larger hotel; Golden had no clue which one, nor did she care, it was part of the adventure and she needed brown liquor ASAP! Golden was the first to exit the SUV, then Tatiana, and lastly, the handsome stranger. The valet gently grasped her hand, then Tatiana's, helping them safely exit the SUV. Golden quickly looked back at the stranger to see if he tipped the valet. She knew if he were generous to the waitstaff, then he would be more than generous with them. She noted the stranger pulled out a money clip and tipped the valet fifty dollars. Golden caught the glimpse of the stranger because he was watching her as well. She pursed her lips and raised an eyebrow in approval of his generosity. Golden's instincts kicked in as she seductively climbed the few steps to the entrance of the hotel as her mesh metallic dress swished over her curves. The bellhop opened the glass door and his eyes widened in delight as he got an up-close view of her. He nodded, addressed her as, "Miss," and guided her to safety all the way into the entrance of the hotel. Golden was pleasantly greeted by marbled floors and the smell of fresh flowers arranged throughout the lobby in various corners and tables. A piano could even be heard in the distance, although Golden couldn't see it. The stranger, without looking, bent his arms for Golden and Tatiana to grab ahold. Golden loved how expensive heels sounded on marble flooring; the sound was unmistakable. The click of her heels mixed with the soft swaying of her metallic dress was absolutely melodic. The trio glided across the lobby toward the hotel bar. As they walked, Golden looked straight ahead but was cognizant of her surroundings. She noticed the eyes of other hotel patrons glancing up from conversations and hotel employees distracted from their duties watching the trio take center stage. Golden felt exhilarated! This was the feeling she craved. She loved the lustful stares from some and the envious stares from others. The attention made her accentuate the sway of her hips even more. Every now and then, she would lick her lips and notice the uncomfortable shift of a group of businessmen in the lobby. She felt their thoughts leaving and their animalistic nature taking over in an instant. She gave a sly smile because that shift in their stances meant blood rushing to their groin, lust having its way. She knew all too well the questioning looks the trio received, but she didn't care because she craved the scrutiny, no matter the perception!

The trio made their way to the bar and began drinking, laughing, and attempting to seduce each other. Golden was a pro at seduction; she learned first-hand watching her mother do it and perfected it at Club V. She intuitively knew her role as Tatiana's wing man. The drinks flowed at the bar as the two beautiful women commanded the attention of the room. "Excuse us, we need to go to the restroom," Tatiana politely announced to the handsome stranger. The two got up and sensually sauntered away with all eyes following them out of the bar and into the lobby. As soon as Tatiana and Golden got inside of the restroom the two fell into a heap of laughter into each other's arms. They laughed uncontrollably, drunk with laughter, alcohol, and greed.

"Oh my god, girl, I'm so glad you decided to come. I missed you so much," Tatiana gushed over Golden.

"Yeah, I'm glad I came too, girl, you out here doing it! For a minute I thought you were out here being a whole sugar baby! I was just trying to figure out, what is happening to my girl?"

"Naw, girl, you already know I get to the bag." Then Tatiana jumped and ran into the bathroom stall as her bladder reminded her why she wanted to come here in the first place. Golden turned and faced the mirror to reapply nude lipstick from her favorite makeup line and apply fresh setting powder. She admired her own beauty in the mirror, adjusted her breasts so they sat just right in her dress, and moved her head side to side, watching her bangs slide across her forehead. She heard Tatiana flush and make her way to the sink. After washing her hands, Tatiana brought out a tiny golden vial, opened it, and took a snort. Golden looked at Tatiana's reflection in the mirror with her mouth agape. She watched her friend take drugs for the first time.

Tatiana tilted her head back enjoying the rush. She'd almost forgotten Golden was there. "Ummm...you want some?" Tatiana asked nervously and washed her hands again, forgetting she already had.

"Hell, no! And Tati, what the fuck are you thinking? Fucking coke, bitch! What?" Golden couldn't believe what her eyes just saw as her brain tried to process Tatiana snorting cocaine or whatever it was.

"Fuck you, bitch! Don't sit on your high and mighty horse like you better than me with yo' drunk ass momma and dead daddy. You should be getting high too!" The last words stuck in Tatiana's throat because she knew she'd gone too far.

Golden's mouth fell open as she shook her head in disbelief. She turned on her heels and started for the door. She reached for the door handle but halted and viciously turned to face Tatiana. Tears swelled in Golden's eyes. "Really, Tati? You talk about my momma and my daddy?" The words stung so bad that Golden felt the bile in her stomach rise into her throat.

"Wait, Golden...wait! I'm sorry...I'm sorry! I didn't mean it." Tatiana ran over to the bathroom door and slammed her hand against it to block Golden's exit.

"Naw, you meant that shit! One thing I learned from my drunk-ass momma is that your true feelings always come out. You know what they say? A drunk mind speak sober thoughts." Golden squared her shoulders, fully facing Tatiana, their faces now merely inches apart. "I never thought my best friend would go so low," Golden said and shut her eyes tightly, fighting back her tears.

"Wait, Golden! I'm sorry. I'm high and drunk! I thought you were judging me. I saw the look in your eyes, and I just lashed out! Wait! Please don't leave me." Tatiana's words stuck in her throat. Golden paused.

Golden's demeanor softened. "Drugs though, Tati? Why?" Golden folded her arms, waiting for her friend to answer.

Tatiana turned around and fell into a heap as she discovered a velvet, plush couch in the bathroom sitting room. Her heart was racing, and she felt like her legs were no longer strong enough to hold her own weight. Golden let out a sigh and fell in a heap beside her friend. "How long, Tati?"

"I can't even remember when I started. Maybe around my sophomore year in high school, and other drugs in my junior year when I dropped out. A mix between coke, heroin, and meth. I drank a lot then used weed to calm my high. My damn mom was a hoe and crackhead, and I never knew my daddy. I had to do what I had to do to numb myself and survive in these streets. I been fucked up my whole life, Golden, I'm not like you. I don't have a grandmother who loves me. All I have is a pretty face and I know how to use it. Sometimes it gets hard, and I just use to take the edge off, ya' know? Look I didn't mean what I said, for real, Golden, you are like the only friend I have." The two sat in silence for a moment letting the bathroom elevator music play in the background of their thoughts.

Golden thought about it and Tatiana was truly the only friend she had too. She didn't approve of her friend getting high and she definitely didn't excuse her talking about her parents either. Golden resigned to the thought of, *No one is perfect, and we all have our crosses.* Golden gave Tatiana a hug. She wanted to trust their friendship and her friend's words about the drugs, but something in the back of her mind knew better. "Let's get back out there, I know my date is waiting. You cool?" Tatiana asked Golden.

The night went on with an air of strain to it. Golden didn't feel like partying anymore and Tatiana could feel it. She explained to the stranger that her friend wasn't feeling well, which wasn't too hard to sell since Golden's smile was long gone after their trip to the bathroom. The stranger said he understood, and Tatiana offered him a free raincheck. Golden wondered what the word *free* entailed.

The handsome stranger called a car service and the pair drove home in silence. Golden pretended to sleep to avoid any more uncomfortable apologies from Tatiana. She needed a moment to process the night's events. *Why would she say that about my momma and daddy?* Golden thought on the drive back to the silver fox's mansion. Golden placed her palms tightly together between her thighs, turned her head toward the corner of the seat, and deeply inhaled the soft, leather seats. Now her metallic dress only made her feel a chill and a little ridiculous considering the evening's sobering events. She felt Tatiana's soft touch wake her as they perched atop the Vegas lights. They seemed a little less bright that night.

Chapter Sixteen

TOOTED UP

The next morning Golden awoke desperately wanting to talk to her grandmother. She needed to hear the comfort of her voice and wisdom about how to react to the things Tatiana told her the previous evening. She reached over and grabbed her phone from the bedside table to turn it on. *Damn it*! She thought, slamming her phone down. She forgot her phone wouldn't power due to its water damage. Golden forcefully turned from her side onto her back, staring at the ceiling, attempting to force her mind to go blank. She didn't want to think about her friend doing drugs in front of her. Nor did she want to think about the hurtful words her best friend uttered about her parents. Tatiana knew how much Golden suffered at the hands of her mother's rageful rants. She never thought she would be on the receiving end of one of those same rants from her best friend.

Golden heard a light tap on her bedroom door. "Come in." She sat up and saw that it was Tatiana. "I was just trying to call my grandmother but remembered my phone is broke," she said as she tossed her useless phone back onto the nightstand.

"Oh, yeah. I remembered you said your phone wasn't working and wanted to bring a peace offering," Tatiana responded, taking her hands from behind her back, holding a new cell phone. She hurried over to Golden's bedside before she could respond. "Look, I was way out of line last night. I shouldn't have said those things about your parents. And I shouldn't have involved you in my bullshit with my client. I kinda look at you like a little sister and I never wanna make you angry or sad. And I didn't want you to see the fucked-up parts of me." Tatiana looked away to avoid Golden's piercing stare and pushed the phone in her direction to create space between the two of them.

"Thank you," Golden replied and took the phone. "We need to talk though. And no more secrets, okay? I gotchu!"

Tatiana nodded.

"So...tell me, what's going on in this house? Does your man know you go out and have...clients?" Golden asked but already knew the answer.

"Ummm...it's complicated, G," Tatiana hesitated. She only called Golden "G" when she was withholding information or telling half-truths.

"C'mon, Tati! We just talked about this, right? No more secrets!" Golden whined.

"Okay...okay." Tatiana stood up, walked to the doorway of Golden's room, peeked outside, and then closed the door. "No more secrets, right? And no judgement?"

Golden nodded in agreement.

"Well...see...he's my pimp." Tatiana avoided Golden's eyes and kept talking because she knew if she stopped then she wouldn't get everything out. "I met him when I was like fourteen and my momma was on drugs. He saw me hanging out, told me I was pretty, and told me he could help me make some money. He taught me everything I know about the game. I started trickin' out of hotel rooms and setting up dates online, just a few here and there 'cause I was still in school. Then the money got good, and I just stopped going to school. Then I kinda started living with him in a different hotel room and partying. I started getting older and growing titties so my man said I should start working in strip clubs. I got real good at it and the clubs started to be my main hustle. One thing led to another and here I am." Tatiana picked at a hang nail as it started to bleed onto the side of her beautiful manicure. The two fell silent for a moment.

"Damn, Tati, I never knew. So, that man has been your…pimp," Golden whispered, "since you were fourteen?"

"Naw, girl, my momma stabbed him, and he died. I met this guy when I moved here. He's been really good to me. Introduced me to some high rollers. He don't put his hands on me and keeps me looking good, whatever I need."

"Including drugs," Golden scoffed, then quickly regretted that last statement. "Well, I'm glad you told me so now I know what's going on."

"I just didn't want you to come here and look down on me, G. This is actually the best life I've ever lived. I'm young, beautiful, and got hella money!"

"Yeah, but you sellin' ass for a nigga!" Golden hissed.

"Look, that may be true, but at least I'm getting paid for it. A lot of these young hoes out here fuckin' for meals or a pair of gym shoes. When I lay down on my back it's for thousands at a time!"

Golden pondered Tatiana's words. She couldn't argue with the lifestyle her friend was living because she'd seen it first-hand. She knew Tatiana was a hustler and businesswoman—probably the best she'd ever seen, and now she knew why. Tatiana didn't have it easy, and she made the best out of a dismal situation. Golden just wanted her friend safe and happy.

"Look, call your granny and check on her. I have to run a couple of errands. Maybe you can meet me at the club tonight where I'm head-lining. You could do my makeup." Tatiana titled her head and made a pouty face, batting her eyelashes so that Golden couldn't refuse."

They both giggled in unison. "You know I got you, girl," Golden replied.

"You can either wear what you brought or go shopping in my closet for a fit, it's up to you." Tatiana shrugged and made her exit. She stopped, turned, and said, "Oh and the car will be here at nine to pick you up." Tatiana blew a kiss to Golden and walked out of the room, shutting the door behind her.

Golden sat for a few moments soaking in the conversation she had had with Tatiana. Then her thoughts quickly turned to her grand-mother. She needed to call her before she went out for the night. Golden turned on the brand-new phone Tatiana gave her, waited for it to power up, and noticed there was only a five percent battery charge. *Just enough to check on her,* Golden thought.

Golden dialed her grandmother's house number. She calculated what time it was at home and figured her grandmother would be right by the phone because her stories were on. Grandmother had her whole lineup of daytime soap operas, westerns, and judge shows to round out the afternoon before she started to cook for the day. The phone rang without an answer. *That's weird,* Golden thought. *Oh well, she might be in the bathroom or something.* Golden left a message, hung up the cell phone, and laid it on the nightstand. She felt better after leaving the message because she knew her grandmother checked voicemails religiously and would feel better knowing Golden was alright.

Golden decided to wear an ensemble she brought instead of wear-ing something from Tatiana's closet. If she was going to be in a foreign environment, then she was going to present as a version of her most authentic self. Golden decided on an all-white look. She knew her dress would look amazing under the black lighting of the club. She loved the juxtaposition of crisp white on her dark skin; she thought it made her look like an angel warrior. She decided to go with all bronze makeup. Golden dug through her hair bag to find inspiration, and she decided on a long, wavy wig with a middle part. The wig's length was right above Golden's waistline. The hair was perfect because it covered Golden's back, and when she turned her head ever so slightly, her hair revealed the backless dress. Golden didn't want to wear an expensive outfit because she knew that drinks could get spilled on her while at a strip club, but she also wanted to make a statement when she entered any room.

Golden packed her makeup bag, double-checking to make sure she had everything needed to create whatever look Tatiana was in the mood for. It took Golden several hours to get ready. It was almost eight o'clock and she wanted to be ready for the driver in case they arrived early. Golden also want to grab a quick bite to eat before heading to the club. She decided to try to call her grandmother one more time before she left for the club. Golden picked up the phone and realized she hadn't put the phone on the charger. "Damn it!" She grabbed the charger out of the box, looking at it, dismayed. Golden grabbed her bags and headed toward the front door, hoping she didn't encounter anyone, particularly Tatiana's pimp. She was slightly annoyed that Tatiana didn't warn her she had a pimp before coming to Vegas. Golden heard too many stories of women having boyfriends-turned-pimps who simply lived off the woman's hard work, and she became nauseous thinking about fourteen-year-old Tatiana in random hotel rooms, having sex with dirty old men. Golden made up her mind that she would never be left alone in the house without Tatiana. She'd seen and heard enough over the years to know that a pimp was bad news, and there may be a possibility that Tatiana's "man" may try Golden and she had to be ready to go at a moment's notice. Golden refused to be any man's whore.

Golden was completely satisfied with her look, despite being distracted by thoughts of Tatiana and her pimp. She checked the time and headed for the front door. As she grabbed the handle and was about to step through it, she heard a voice coming from behind her. "Leaving so soon?" Golden held her breath and slightly turned her body to make eye contact with Tatiana's pimp.

"Yeah, I was just leaving to meet Tati. She's waiting on me." Every hair on Golden's body raised as the man slowly walked toward her. He seemed to enjoy watching Golden squirm. Golden gave an awkward giggle, nodded, and started out the front door. "Okay, bye."

Golden almost had the heavy, ornate door closed. She could even see her driver standing, waiting for her with the door open. Then she heard the man call after her, "Golden." It was the way he called her name that made her body tense. She only had one other encounter where she felt that unsafe, and another chill went through her as her body remembered the terror. Golden turned her head in response to her name being called.

The man held a wad of money in a gold-plated clip. "Could you give this to Tatiana when you see her?" In two swift steps, the man was so close to Golden that she could see the wrinkles in his forehead emerging through his tanned, leathery skin.

"Sure." Golden tried to quickly grab the clip of money, but the man snatched it back just out of Golden's reach. He stepped uncomfortably close and invaded Golden's personal space. He moved his head from one side to the other like a snake, confusing Golden. He was close enough to brush his lips on her face, moving his head from side to side. Golden fought the urge to turn her face to the side to avoid his advance. She stood frozen, hardened her eyes, and stared straight into his. She held his gaze for a moment, lifting her chin, slightly angling her body to be square with his. The pimp let out a light snort of air through his nose, smirked, and handed Golden the money clip full of cash. As she tried to take it, the man tightened his grip and slowly uttered, "You have stunning eyes, my dear." Then he loosened his grip on the money clip. Golden tightened her jaw and slowly took the money clip, opened the door, and walked to her ride.

Once inside of the car, Golden broke down crying and gasping for air. She was so frightened and angry. Firstly, she was angry at herself because she never asked Tatiana detailed questions about her lifestyle. Secondly, she was furious at Tatiana for inviting her into her crazy lifestyle and leaving her alone with a predator and pimp. Lastly, she was mad at the pimp because he assumed, she too, could be bought. Golden slammed her head into the back of the seat to calm herself and still her tears. Her driver eyed her worriedly in the rearview mirror. When they made eye contact, Golden said, "I'm fine, please just drive. You have the address, right?" He nodded. "And do you have a phone charger?" The driver silently handed Golden a charger while eyeing her through the rearview mirror.

"Excuse me…Miss, we're here," the driver said. Golden had fallen asleep and awoke with a start and gasped. "You're okay, you're okay," the driver reassured her. Golden sat in the back seat and closed her eyes tightly. She felt her new phone vibrate but didn't look at the screen because the only person who had her number was Tatiana. Golden sat still, replaying the events with Tatiana's pimp. "Hey, you wanna go somewhere?"

The driver's invitation rocked her out of her own wind tunnel of emotions. "Yes," she thought. She wanted to be anywhere but in a loud club, and in the presence of Tatiana, nonetheless. She looked at her phone and it was Tatiana asking where she was. Golden lied and texted that she was going to get something to eat before coming to the club. Then Golden noticed her phone was only on five percent. Her phone hadn't been charging. The driver repeated himself. "You wanna go somewhere and get something to eat?"

"Go where?" Golden asked as she tried to remember if she plugged in her phone. She remembered the driver had handed her his charger through the partition, but she didn't actually see it plugged in.

"Ummm...wherever you wanna go. This was my last ride of the day. I only have to do one of these kinds of drives and it usually pays for my whole shift, then some." The driver stared at Golden in the rearview mirror, waiting for her answer.

Her mind was racing; she didn't know who to trust or where to go. She was in a city where she didn't know anyone but her best friend, and now, even she seemed like a stranger. Golden sat motionless while her brain ran in circles, processing every moment, everything Tatiana ever told her. She felt a small headache starting to form in her left temple. Then her stomach audibly growled. The driver laughed.

"Shoot, you may wanna get something to eat. I know a place not far from here, a burger joint."

Golden shot the driver a questioning look. She regretted being in Vegas. She was without her mace, her taser, and her small.22 she normally carried all the time. She felt so vulnerable and indefensible. "Look, I'mma be honest with you. I ain't got time for no bullshit, alright. So, if you plan on raping me or kidnapping me, just do it now, don't wait." Then she slammed her head to the back of the seat and closed her eyes, mentally preparing for an attack.

"Yo, shawty, I don't know what you been through, but that definitely ain't me. Now I can drop yo' ass off here like I was paid to do, or you can act like you got some fuckin' sense when somebody is trying to be nice to you."

Golden opened her eyes and stared at the driver in the rearview. "My bad, I just had a rough couple days out here, don't know who the fuck to trust."

"It's all good, I got you. Look, how about you text whoever you was texting and send them your location and share your route."

That was actually a really good idea. However, Golden quickly sent a text to one of the only cell phone numbers she knew by heart: Marquez.

> *Hey, this is Golden. My new number. Out in Vegas, gonna share my route so I don't get kidnapped.*

She hit send. "Okay, where to, Mr. Driver?" Golden asked in a condensing tone.

"I'm gonna take you to my uncle's spot. It ain't real fancy but it's nice."

Golden nodded. She needed to feel like she was in motion and not sitting still because when she did, she flashed back to Tatiana's pimp approaching her. She had seen girls in strip club after strip club get mixed up with men calling themselves pimps. In Golden's eyes, all they were to her were insecure men who couldn't make a living on their own merit and had to degrade and manipulate a woman to sell her body so he could survive. Golden felt a chill run across the tops of her arms, and goosebumps prickled in response. She sat very still, quickly glanced at the driver in the mirror, and noticed his right eye flinch as he began to reach for the gear shift. Golden could hear Althea's voice in her head, *Watch these niggas out here, everybody got a tell.*

That meant that people's body language would give their subcon-scious thoughts away before their words or actions would. Golden quickly reached for the door handle, grabbing her small purse, and was hitting her heels to pavement before the driver realized what was happening. "Aye, come back here!" The driver shouted after her. She heard the SUV door close behind her and the heavy footsteps of the driver give chase. They were behind the building of the club so no one could hear or see her right now. Golden knew the only chance she had to escape whatever fate the driver planned for her was to be around as many witnesses as possible. All Golden could think was *Faster, faster!*

As she neared the edge of the back alley, she saw a few pedestri-ans and scantily clad girls walking to the club entrance. "Help!" she shouted, but her cries were drowned out by the growing intensity of the club's music. She heard the man's footsteps quicken behind her. "Fire!" She yelled at the top of her lungs. Just then a group of three women heard her yell over the music and their laughs, and they paused to look in the direction of the warning. The driver knew the chase was over. "You lucky bitch!" She could hear his retreating footsteps and breathlessly continued towards the confused girls.

"Thank you. Thank you for stopping." Golden quickly walked past the group of women, and as soon as she rounded the corner, she saw the worried face of Tatiana standing outside.

"Golden!" Tatiana ran toward her friend in a panic. She'd never seen Golden look disheveled and distraught. Tatiana moved passed security and embraced Golden as she fell into her arms in a heap. "I'm sorry, G...I'm sorry. Did he? Never mind, let's get you inside to the bathroom." Tatiana quickly ushered Golden past security. She could feel Golden shaking. Tatiana knew she had to get Golden somewhere safe, and fast. The two walked for a moment and then Tatiana parted a pair of curtains that were hidden behind a huge column. Behind the column was a black door with a digital keypad that Tatiana entered a code into, waited for the beep, and then entered. Once the door was closed, the music and people instantly became muffled. They both entered a small room with a mirror and one plush bench. Just opposite from the door was another door, but Tatiana stopped before opening that door and sat Golden down. "G! I'm so sorry. I should've never left you there alone. I knew you could handle yourself, but I also saw how he looked at you when I first showed him pictures of you. I knew he wanted you and my dumb ass still brought you here. Please forgive me, G!"

"Wait...what?" Golden stammered. "What are you talking about, Tati? You mean you knew that man wanted to pimp me out and you invited me down here? Still?" Golden's mouth dropped open in disbelief. Golden's question hung in the air unanswered. The silence was piercing until Tatiana broke.

"I wanted us to be real sisters, G!"

Golden shook her head, not understanding Tatiana's statement. "Neither one of us have any brothers or sisters. Both of our mommas ain't shit, and daddies" Tatiana's voice trailed off. She got down on one knee in front of Golden and grabbed both of her hands. Partly because she wanted Golden's attention and partly because she didn't want Golden to slap her for trying to turn her to prostitution. "I know, I know, G! I fucked up! I should've just been straight from the beginning and told you everything. I just wanted someone to share my life with, a real sister. Someone who would have my back and really love me. I ain't never had that. You are the closest thing to it."

Golden flared her nostrils and let out a quick breath. She clinched her fist tight because the urge to slap and punch Tatiana was almost too great for her to resist. "I'm as real as they come, Tati. My momma's a hoe and Daddy died a drug dealer. Nobody wanted to be my friend growing up because of that. Or I couldn't trust girls my own age because they was jealous and the boys just wanted to fuck. The only person to ever love me was my grandmother. She was the only one; the only one to love on me and encourage me that I was more than the daughter of a hoe and drug dealer. She made me believe I could be more. Then you come along and pretended to be my friend. Naw, I take that back, you don't know shit about being a friend. You drew me in with the money 'cause you knew I was looking for a way out. And I thank you for teaching me the game. But I ain't fuckin' for no dollas, T! You tryna turn me into my momma or worse...yours!"

Tatiana stood from the weight and shock of Golden's words and started to back away from Golden. She noticed the change in color of Golden's eyes from a pretty, light green tint to hazel, just like Althea's. Tatiana could feel the fiery hate bubbling like lava out of Golden. Tatiana tried to step away from Golden, but the room was so small. As Tatiana shrank, Golden stood up slowly, fists clutched, and fire in her eyes.

"Is there a problem, ladies?" A cool voice cooed from the opposite door they had entered. The two women hadn't noticed the door nearest them opening. It was Tatiana's pimp dressed in a white button down long-sleeve shirt with tailored black trousers. Two large men loomed behind him, dressed in all black. He flashed his white veneers and extended his hands toward the two women. "Shall we retire to my office?" The man had a quiet strength that didn't lend itself to hearing *no*. The two women both took a half step back from each other while their eyes searched the floor like two teenagers getting in trouble for arguing over something trivial. Golden turned and grabbed her purse from the bench and followed Tatiana through the door of the room. She wasn't afraid of the pimp; Golden needed space between her and Tatiana.

CHAPTER SEVENTEEN

BLOOD CONTRACT

Tatiana and Golden followed the pimp into an all-black office and sat near each other in soft, leather chairs, just in front of a large, looming desk in the center of the room where the pimp took centerstage. Golden's anger toward Tatiana was quelled for a moment as she silently took in her immediate surrounds. The entire office was black. Plush, black carpet stifled the sound of their stilettos. As Golden squinted, she could see black wallpaper with a paisley print to accent the black matte finish. In the center of the room was a black wooden desk with a golden trim. The room was stunning.

"I think we got off on the wrong foot, Golden. May I call you Golden?"

Golden nodded.

"And you may call me G," he said.

Golden watched G move across the room like a lynx circling his prey. He stood at the corner of his desk and opened an ornate box gilded in embossed gold detailing. He reached for a cigar, rolled it between his fingers, and held it to his nose to savor its sweet fragrance while his eyes hungrily fixated on Tatiana. She noticeably shifted in her seat underneath the weight of his gaze. Golden realized she never saw the two interact together in a nonsocial situation. She paid attention. She had to know how this man had such a mental hold over her friend.

G began to methodically go through the process of lighting his cigar while he spoke. Each syllable was measure and each word was thought out. G didn't use any extra words to express his thoughts. "Tatiana told me a lot about you when she was on her Midwest tour. She told me that you had a hustle about you, and you weren't impressed with the shiny things this industry brings." He stopped to light his cigar by striking a match from the cigar box on his desk, puckering his lips into a tight circle, and he took three smacking puffs to ignite the cigar. G leaned back into his chair, satisfied at the quality of his cigar. He paused to look at it, almost forgetting he was talking, and then he continued.

"Tatiana never had any sisters growing up and her momma wasn't shit," G added matter-of-factly. "She been my main woman since the age of sixteen." G kept talking, averting eye contact with Golden and Tatiana. "When I met her, she was standing at a bus stop, already hoeing but doing it wrong, basically giving that pussy away for free."

Golden steadied her breath. She tried to stay calm while listening to this predator talk about her friend and how he turned her out. Golden remembered conversations with her mother about pimps and hoes. Althea told Golden that a pimp was a coward: messing with women's heads to do something they would never have the courage or balls to do themselves.

"I know you ain't no hoe or prostitute," G said and paused for effect, looking up at Golden through a cloud of smoke. "But I also know you about yo' bread." G rested his cigar in a black ceramic boat and continued. "I wanna make you a business proposition." G folded his hands and looked intently at Golden to make sure he had her full attention.

Golden was intrigued. She fully expected G to try to run game on her and coax her into prostitution by saying it's a family and they have to watch out for each other. That he can offer her protec-tion...blah...blah...blah. She was expecting him to exploit her fractured relationship with her mother and the untimely death of her father to crack her hardened exterior. But he didn't, and that made Golden lean in further with curiosity.

"Look, I run several businesses. I am a businessman and one thing I know how to do is see a need and fill it with the right product or service. And I think you have just the right piece to a missing puzzle I've been trying to solve. I am starting an escort business."

Tatiana quickly glanced at Golden to measure her reaction. Tatiana was taken aback because G promised Tatiana she was going to be the head of his new escort business venture. She couldn't hide her confusion and started to protest when G shot her a menacing look. Tatiana quickly rethought her approach. She tightly gripped the arms of the cool, black leather chair and inched her back toward the seat.

G went on and ignored Tatiana's confused gaze. "I know you and Tatiana are friends and I never wanna come between you two, but this is business. Right, baby?" G looked over at Tatiana and she didn't move.

"Here's how I see it. You have been stripping and doing shows in your area. Small potatoes. You ain't seen money yet. I know Tatiana told you about the contracted club tours she does. Well, I made that happen for her. Taught her the game and she flipped it and made it her own. Now my baby brings in damn near a half million just on those contracts alone, not including tips and her other private clients."

This was the first time Golden looked at Tatiana. She could now see past all the makeup, designer clothes, thirty-inch extensions, and air of confidence. As Golden looked at her friend, now she saw the real Tatiana: a scared little girl just trying to make her way in this heartless world. Golden caught the lump in her throat that was forming and swallowed it down to find her voice.

"And why the hell should I go into business with you?" Golden spat out at G, trying to gain dominance over the conversation. One thing she learned from Althea, passed down from Mother Rose, was that a man is always gonna want what a woman has to offer; you just gotta figure out the price he's willing to pay for it.

G gave a half smile. "So, now we in negotiations?"

They both sat and stared at each other, playing mental chess, sizing up one another, trying to figure out the other's weaknesses and angles.

G finally broke the stare off. "Look, Golden, I ain't even gonna play with you. I see what I want and I gotta have it. But I'm honest about mine. I know it costs to be with a woman of your caliber." G paused; he knew he laid on the compliment too thick because he saw Golden's eyes narrow with contempt. He knew that he had to be honest with this one. No games could be played: she knew all of them. Someone had taught her well.

"Lemme just lay it out. I'm starting a high-end escort service of exotic women only. Do you know what exotic means? Just not women who look good, but who are intelligent and can talk a man outta anything, even his wedding ring if she wants it. Most of these men with power want to be dominated. They don't want that weak bitch he got at home. He wants excitement and that's what I'm selling. Fantasy."

"What's my role and what's my cut?" Golden asked coolly.

G sat back in his large leather chair, pleased that negotiations were going so well as a soft smile played around the corners of his mouth. "Seventy/thirty," G stated in an even tone.

"And you bring me on as the creative director. I curate the girls, their looks, the fantasy. I'm thinking a huge mansion that can be a members-only club. But I ain't fuckin', suckin', or dancin'." Golden tilted her head, crossed her long legs, and folded her manicured hands in her lap, awaiting G's answer.

"Sounds interesting. I will have you meet with my lawyer tomorrow to draw up an agreement about the particulars. You can work out the details with him. Whatever you ask, I'm agreeable." G nodded.

Tatiana sat in her seat in disbelief. G never gave her a cut of anything. And she never saw G give in so easily during a deal. *Ever!* She gave all her money to him, all except for the tips she made at her club appearance. Even her club contract fees went directly into an account that only G had access to. *Why am I being treated like a fucking whore?* she thought. *Why don't I get to be in charge? I've paid my dues! Hell, half my life has been spent making this man rich and what do I have to show for it?* Tatiana was furious and equally confused.

"I'll have the driver take you two ladies home. Golden, the lawyer will meet you at the house tomorrow at noon to draft our contract." G stood and the outside door to the office opened, letting in the music from the club.

The pair were ushered through the club to a town car waiting out front. When they were both inside, Tatiana quickly shifted her whole body to face Golden. "I can't fucking believe you, bitch! Really? You go into business with my man?"

"And I can't believe you either, bitch! You brought me here to hoe me out! Oh...what, you think I didn't know? It started to make sense when you left me home alone with that nigga. And you knew he was gonna push up on me. And if I hadn't made a power move I woulda been lying on my fucking back just like you cuz he don't look like the type to take no for an answer."

The two fell silent in the back seat. Tatiana knew she was right. G wanted Golden as soon as he saw video of her from one of her dances. He fixated on Golden and asked Tatiana all types of questions about her home life, upbringing, and personality. Tatiana knew he was trying to find an angle to make Golden a piece of his property. *Damn, how could I let this happen to my friend?* Tatiana thought while guilt shrouded her in darkness for the remainder of the silent ride home.

※※※※

The next morning Golden awoke to the beaming Vegas sunshine pouring into her room. She had forgotten to completely close the blackout curtains when she got home. Golden yawned and quickly remembered to call her grandmother. Her new phone should have been completely charged by then.

The phone rang more times than usual. She figured her grandmother would be up by now, given the time difference. She held the phone impatiently waiting for someone to pick up on the other end. "Hello." It was Grandmother's voice, but it sounded unfamiliar.

"Hey Grandma, it's me, Golden."

"Hold on, baby, lemme sit up. Who is this?"

"Grandma, it's me, Golden. I was calling to check on you."

"Golden?" Grandmother's voice sounded so weak and far away. Golden started to feel an immense sense of dread swell in the pit of her stomach.

"Yeah, Grandma, it's me. How you been?"

"I...I'm tired baby, just in the bed resting."

Golden instantly knew something was wrong. Her grandmother was usually up by then, washing clothes and cleaning up breakfast dishes while watching her favorite morning news shows.

"Baby, I'm so glad to hear from you. How's Vegas? And how's Tati?"

Oh good; she remembered Golden was in Vegas and who she was there with. That made Golden settle into her bed and put her mind at ease.

"Things are good here, Grandma. I'm starting a business. I think I may get to do some styling and creative directing for a big show out here in Vegas," Golden half-lied.

"That's good, baby, just make sure they pay you. You know Vegas is full of crooks at every turn. You go there thinking you gonna win and end up getting played. You know what they say, the house always wins. And don't nobody beat the house for too long." Grandma then let out a dry cough.

"Grandma, you don't sound too good."

"I'm fine, baby, you don't worry about me. My throat's just dry. I'm 'bout to get up from this here bed and check on my beans. You know I like to get 'em started early."

Beans and cornbread sounded so good right then. Golden could taste the savory beans and sweet, honey cornbread that only her grandmother knew how to make, just as she liked it.

"Well, I'm gonna let you go, Grandma. I got business to take care of today."

"Okay, baby. I'm so proud of you. My baby following her dreams." Grandmother's voice trailed off. Then she cleared her throat. "Just know when to leave the table, baby. I told yo' daddy that and he didn't listen. This game don't love nobody. Promise...here? Don't stay too long."

"I won't," Golden replied. "I love you and I'll call you in a few days to check up on you." Just then Golden heard the banging of the screen door in the background and knew Althea must be home. Golden tried to rush off the phone. "Okay, Grandmother, I'm gonna call you in a few days. And take my new number down so you can call me if you need anything." Golden didn't hear a reply. However, she did hear Althea approaching.

"Is that Golden on the phone? Lemme speak to her."

Golden let out a loud sigh and her eyes rolled in the back of her head. Althea was the last thing she needed this morning, right before an important meeting.

"Hello...Golden?"

"Hey," Golden replied dryly.

"That money you left is all gone. How you just gonna leave me and your grandmother here like that? Bills need to be paid and we need food too."

Golden knew that the house was paid for and that her grandmother received government assistance for food and a stipend for household goods. She knew that Althea had expensive tastes and a drinking problem, but she also didn't want her to have to degrade herself for it.

"I'm gonna send you some money to your account right now. I got a new phone so give me a minute to set it up."

"Well, my account is negative so you gonna have to add a lil' extra in there to cover it plus the money you was gonna send." Althea was never good at managing her money. She simply spent whatever money she got as she received it. There were many days when they went without food, lights, and water because of Althea's irresponsible habits. Golden started taking care of all the household bills at fifteen and put everything in her name.

Talking to Althea made Golden's head throb harder than it already did. She rubbed her forehead, asking Althea, "So, how much you short?"

"Bout $500. Yup, we need about $500. Make it $800 cuz I need to go to the store too," Althea lied. But Golden couldn't tell her no. She knew her mother couldn't function on her own. The person she really worried about was her grandmother. Golden didn't want her to suffer while she was in Vegas.

"And where the hell you at anyway?"

"I'm in Vegas, Momma."

"Ohhhhh, so you a fuckin' high roller now, huh? Well, make it an even $1,000 cuz you ain't coming back for a few days, I know."

"Okay, Momma." The last thing Golden wanted to do was argue. Then she heard the dial tone. Typical Althea. She got what she wanted and then went ghost.

Golden quickly changed over her account number to sync with her new phone number and sent $1,500 to Althea's account. That way she knew that her grandmother would have food to eat. Then Golden paid all the household bills before getting in the shower. Her meeting was in twenty minutes, and she needed to be on her game. Golden assembled her outfit in her head the night before, so it was easy to quickly get dressed.

When Golden opened the door to her room, the housekeeper was waiting outside. Golden instinctively followed her through several parts of the house she had yet to visit until they arrived at a pair of black double doors. The housekeeper gently knocked on the doors and opened them without hesitation, moving aside for Golden to enter. Inside, the large room was almost identical to the club office Golden visited the night before except this office was all white instead of black. The office contained a small desk with a laptop and an additional desk in the back left-hand corner of the room. Golden confidently walked into the empty room. She wondered if she had the right time because the office was empty. As she spun around to ask the housekeep about G's whereabouts, the housekeeper quickly exited the room and closed the double doors behind her. Golden stood in front of the doors waiting and listening for some type of movement. She felt her nerves getting the best of her. She noticed a bar along the side of the wall and decided to make a drink. Then she quickly decided against a drink. She needed to be mentally sharp and fully aware of her surroundings. She stood for a moment longer and her feet began to ache.

Golden wanted to impress G, so she wore one of the highest heels she had, paired with tailored, black tuxedo pants that she crafted herself. Her shirt was a black corset bodice paired with a scoop neck that had black chiffon sleeves that billowed out to complement the structure of the corset. *I can't stand too much longer in these shoes,* she thought. She decided to take a seat in front of the desk. As soon as she sat down, the rear office door opened and G appeared with a man behind him looking equally as important. G didn't waste any time. He got straight to business by introducing his lawyer and briefly explaining that his lawyer was going to handle the details of the contract. G would review it later and they would both sign when the agreement was suitable for both parties. Then G quickly excused himself and exited the office through the front door. The lawyer took a seat behind the looming white desk, opening his laptop, and said, "Shall we get started?"

Golden nodded, scooting closer to the edge of her seat. She was very intimidated by G's lawyer because his sentences were very short and to the point and his demeanor was free of pleasantries. He did not laugh at Golden's weak attempts at jokes, nor did he smile while he gathered her information to begin the contract.

"So, what do you want to get out of this arrangement, Miss?" The lawyer asked Golden. It was the first time he looked up from his laptop, meeting her green eyes with his deep brown. Golden was instantly stuck because the lawyer's eyes were wide and engaging. She felt as if he could see straight into her thoughts, and she couldn't lie.

She started to stutter, "I..I..I want it all."

The lawyer raised one eyebrow, curious at the young woman's answer. He was used to being lied to. It was rare that someone showed all their intentions right away. "What do you mean, Miss, by "all"?"

The question made Golden stammer again. "Ummm."

"What do you want, Miss? If you could do what you love, what would that be?" The lawyer's eyes bore even deeper into Golden's. He was now more intrigued with her follow-up responses to his questions. He'd been G's lawyer for seven years, had seen a lot of G's business dealings, and had gotten him out of legal trouble more times than he cared to count. But G paid him well, and he learned a long time ago not to ask questions. The lawyer sat in this very same room with a number of women and drafted contracts for them to be escorts, bartenders, housekeepers, drivers, and non-disclosures. He knew all of G's business partners, whether the business was legal or illegal. It was the lawyer's job to transform and detail any activity into a legal and binding agreement, and he was very good at his job.

Golden and the lawyer sat at the table for what seemed like hours, negotiating the contract. They worked for so long, the housekeeper interrupted by bringing them lunch. They continued to talk, eat, and draft the contract. Golden felt invigorated and energized after the delicious lunch, and she wanted to press on to get the contract finished. With each line of the contract, she felt herself being reinvented. She felt as if the person she always dreamed herself to be was meeting her current self in real-time, and she experienced a moment of pride, watching herself be the boss she always knew was.

She felt the pain of her past, the old version of herself become hazier. Golden felt some of the heartbreak caused by losing her father at a young age mend a little during her time with the lawyer. She felt like her father would be proud of her in this moment because she was choosing herself for once. She didn't consider her alcoholic mother's feelings because she knew that Althea stopped believing in herself years ago. She didn't have anything left in her to give to Golden. She didn't think about how much her grandmother would miss her while she was completing the terms of her contract. However, Golden did think about Mother Rose, who never believed in her all those years ago when she was just a little girl wanting to show off her talent for dress-making. Within a few hours, all the self-confidence that Mother Rose stole during her last prison visit was restored, and Golden beamed with a renewed pride.

Golden and the lawyer negotiated a three-month contract making Golden the creative director of G's escort business. Her main duties included decorating a mansion G already owned. Each room in the mansion would have a theme and the escort occupying that room would match the theme. Each escort would have a costume, hair, and makeup curated by Golden to ensure a cohesive fantasy that matched the décor of the rooms. The lawyer suggested Golden be creative director of the escorts as well as the mansion rooms to ensure cohesion.

"Of course, you will be compensated for the additional duties. Always, ask for compensation." The lawyer nodded in Golden's direction without lifting his eyes from his laptop.

Golden became curious about the lawyer. She wondered how he knew G and what their connection to each other was. "So, if you don't mind me asking, how do you know G?"

The lawyer didn't move his eyes from his laptop screen. Golden thought for a moment that he didn't hear her until he answered, "My relationship with G is none of your business."

Golden let out a puff of air through her nostrils. She thought that she and the lawyer were gaining a rapport with each other, but her hopes were quickly deflated by the way he shot down her curiosity. The two sat in silence again while the lawyer typed and edited the contract. Golden felt the need to fill the silence, embarrassed by the response of the lawyer.

"I met G's girl, Tatiana, at a strip club when I did her makeup," Golden offered as a means of small talk.

The lawyer let out an audible sigh. It was the first time Golden noticed that he showed emotion. Golden interpreted the sigh as boredom until the lawyer spoke.

"No, Miss Rose, you met Tatiana at the mall where you initially did her makeup. Then she hired you to do her makeup at the club." The lawyer stopped, folded his hands, and peered at Golden. "Please understand that I know all of G's business and anyone attached to G. If anyone is in his presence, I know about them first. It would be too risky otherwise. I know exactly who you are and what you specialize in." The lawyer ended flatly.

Golden's head was spinning. Her voice was screaming in her head. *How does the lawyer know the exact circumstances in which I met Tatiana.* Golden decided that small talk was no longer a requirement and only answered specific questions the lawyer asked.

"I will have G look at these documents tonight and he'll make any changes he sees fit. Then I will meet with you again tomorrow to go over those changes. Once an agreement is reached, then the contract will be signed, notarized, and filed with the clerk's office. If anything changes, we will contact you. Do you have any questions?"

"No," Golden answered. Her head was still spinning, trying to figure out exactly who G was and how the lawyer was so knowledgeable about how she met Tatiana. She thanked the lawyer and walked to her room, wondering what else the lawyer knew.

The rest of the evening was uneventful. Golden was so mentally exhausted from her time spent in contract negotiations that she fell asleep fully clothed. She planned to call her grandmother and tell her the good news about her new job and how she'd be creating a whole scene and mood from the ground up.

❉❉❉❉

The housekeeper gently knocked on Golden's door the next morning and told her through the door to meet the lawyer in one hour in the office. Golden scrambled to get ready for the meeting. That day, she searched her wardrobe to find anything that looked less revealing than usual. As she was getting ready, she took one last look in the mirror and didn't recognize herself for a moment. For once, she was meeting up with a man and not focused on her breasts popping out of her top as a means of distraction. She was already getting what she wanted based on her skills, not on her looks. She gave her reflection an approving nod and confidently walked to the office.

The door to the office was open, with G, the lawyer, and another woman she had never seen before, all awaiting her arrival. Golden gave a nervous smile while G ushered her over to a chair opposite him and the lawyer.

"So, I see you and my lawyer were very busy yesterday. He told me that you thought your monthly fee should be higher and you wanted your money all up front." G's eye's searched Golden's eyes.

Golden didn't have a clue what G was talking about. She didn't ask for a rate increase, nor did she ask for her money up front.

"Yes," said the lawyer. "Miss Rose is a very tough negotiator," the lawyer answered in her stead. "So, these are the terms." The lawyer turned a copy of Golden's contract toward her. They all had their own copies and read all the agreed upon terms. And that's when Golden saw it. Her fee stated she would earn $15,000 per month for her duties, to be paid up front. Then she would receive an extra $5,000 incentive pay if her mock-ups of the mansion rooms and escorts' costumes were all sketched and drafted within seven days. Golden thought, *That means I would make $50k in three months!* "Her eyes lifted from her contract and briefly met those of the lawyer. He slightly narrowed his eyes and fixed his gaze intently on Golden's. She intrinsically knew it was his doing, but she wondered why he added the incentives and bonuses to her contract that weren't discussed the day before. Golden's confidence grew and she sat taller, believing in her abilities more and more with each passing moment. The lawyer, G, and Golden reviewed the contract line by line, ensuring both parties' interests were represented. She noted the contract referred to G as *Williams Holdings & Trust*. The other woman in the room kept note of the changes and printed out the final document for G and Golden to sign.

Golden's heart raced as she picked up her pen and signed her name to the contract. The woman checked their identifications and notarized the document. "Okay, Miss Rose, I will file this document with Clark County circuit court tomorrow and will print out a copy for you in just a moment." The woman smiled warmly at Golden. It was the first time Golden heard her speak, and her voice and demeanor set Golden's racing heart at ease.

Golden's heart rate was quickened once more with the sound of G's voice. "In celebration of our upcoming project, I've called a few of my potential clients for the mansion over to the house tonight. I want them to hear your vision and how you plan to customize their fantasies. You can use your imagination, but I'm sure it won't be a stretch to talk to potential customers about their sex fantasies." G gave Golden a crooked smile that nearly took away her joy in an instant.

The lawyer instantaneously sensed Golden's demeanor shift and interrupted G's nasty remark. "Miss Rose," he added softly. "I think our customers will be wowed by your vision, and sometimes creating out loud on the fly helps to get those creativity sparks flying. I have every confidence in you."

"Uhhh...right," Golden stated, looking back and forth from G to the lawyer. For a moment, she saw G's confidence slip, and she finally understood the lawyer was the boss; G was simply the face of his operations. Golden had a knack for reading people; it was something Althea taught her at an early age. Althea also taught her how to read a room for the wrong reasons. She taught Golden how to anticipate a person's actions and how to disarm them with charm. Those were the main skills Mother Rose used to pull off her huge merchandise heists from high-end department stores. *You act like you belong, baby, and then, like clockwork, these dumbasses believe you do.*

Golden cleared her throat and thanked them both for the opportunity. She excused herself, her mind swirling with the thoughts of her bonus, her new job, and being in the career she never dreamed she would ever have. She wanted only to speak to one person: her grandmother. Golden hurried to her room to call her grandmother. The phone rang without an answer. Golden thought it strange, ended the call, and called back again. There was still no answer. Then she remembered it was Sunday. Her grandmother was probably at church and Althea was probably on the couch drunk and passed out from the night before. Golden quickly ended the call, dreading a drunken interaction from her mother. The last thing Golden wanted was for Althea to ruin her good news with personal attacks and negativity.

Golden sometimes wondered if Althea ever wanted her at all. She quickly stood to push those thoughts out of her head. She didn't have any time for a trip down her horrible childhood; she had to get ready for her meet and greet, starting in a few hours.

As Golden searched through her suitcases for a complete head-to-toe look, she found a picture strip of Tatiana and herself taken at an old-school photobooth from one of their crazy nighttime adventures. She longingly looked at the picture and felt a pain in her chest. She had to admit, she missed her friend. So, she decided to call Tatiana.

"Hello!" Tatiana was screaming on the other end over the loud background noise.

"Hey, girl, I was just calling to see what you were doing," Golden yelled back over the noise. "And I wanted to know what you were wearing to tonight's party. I thought we could do a fun little matchy look."

The other end was silent. "Hello? Tati, did you hear me?"

"Yeah, ummm...I can't make it. I'm in Chicago for a gig." Then the call ended.

Chapter Eighteen

Work Ain't Honest

The intro of the party was a success that night, and Golden couldn't wait to get to work on the mansion project. G told Golden he had a downstairs bedroom repurposed as an office for Golden. She loved it but was left to wonder, *When did G have the time to personalize it for me?* She loved that the walls and carpet were all stark white with a blush-colored, textured paint covering the walls. The desk was white with gold hardware and a brand-new laptop, completing the office décor. She was awestruck and grateful that such care was given to personalize her office. Her favorite picture of Grandmother and her, taken from her social media, was on display in a beautiful, ornate frame to match the gold hardware on her desk. Golden felt a warmth surge in her chest at the thought of her grandmother and all the support she showed Golden when she didn't even believe in herself. *If only she could see me now*, Golden thought as she began to feel tears swell in her the corners of her eyes, refusing to let them fall.

Mother Rose calling Golden a "stupid tar baby" and Althea telling her men only want sex from her; thoughts about working all those years at the makeup counter for just above minimum wage, knowing she could do so much more with her talent, but not believing in herself: these now faded into the background. Golden scoffed at the irony that a pimp made good on his promise and made her dreams come true. At this very moment, Golden believed she had the talent and drive to not only be in this space, but to dominate. Grateful tears fell down Golden's cheeks; tears she held back for many years.

Just then, Golden heard a chime from her computer, seeing the face of the lawyer waiting for her to answer the video call. Golden quickly scanned the room for tissue. Luckily, she found some located on a bookshelf in an ornate, golden tissue box holder. She quickly grabbed a few tissues; grateful she had the foresight to wear waterproof mascara.

Golden answered the video chat. "Good morning, Miss Rose," greeted the lawyer in a flat tone, as usual. Golden didn't have time to reply because the lawyer seamlessly started a conversation about the previous night's party, and how the investors were very happy with her vision and eager to see it come to life. Golden got hung up on the word *investors* because she thought the group of people she met that night would be her customers: the ones who would frequent the mansion. Golden had to quickly refocus her energy and concentrate on the lawyer's words because he was talking faster than her thoughts could process.

The lawyer quickly noticed the moment Golden lost focus, and she saw an alert that another user was requesting control of her laptop. The lawyer quickly said, "That's me...accept." Golden complied and the lawyer quickly went through the entire contents of her laptop, showing her where she could find lists of possible contractors, vendors, co-lead interior designers, and every other contact that Golden failed to think of. The lawyer thought of everything, except one thing. Golden was happy for the opportunity, but quickly questioned how she was going to complete everything and get all of her workers chosen, as well as the staff, all by herself.

The lawyer added that he hired an assistant on Golden's behalf, and she should be arriving within the next thirty minutes to help Golden with anything she needed. The lawyer assured Golden that her assistant was fully capable of handling anything Golden may throw at her and urged her to use her wisely. Golden felt a sense of calm overcome her in the storm of chaos.

As if on cue, Golden's assistant, Gia, arrived about twenty-five minutes after the video call with the lawyer ended. Gia was about a foot shorter than Golden with shoulder-length, deep smoldering red hair. Her fair skin tone shone in stark contrast to her hair. Golden learned that Gia just completed her master's degree in business management and this job was a paid internship for her. She was only one year younger than Golden.

Golden immediately felt intimidated by the organization and poise that Gia brought into the room. Golden resigned that Gia would be her ally and reminded herself that she was the boss and Gia was her employee. Golden decided to treat this relationship no different than the other working relationships she had in the past, especially at the makeup counter, training new employees and mentoring new dancers at the V.

Gia came ready to work. She introduced herself and set her laptop on the small desk in the corner of Golden's office. This was the first time Golden even noticed the tiny desk in the corner. She took it as a good sign that Gia would be able to take care of the small details while Golden concentrated her efforts on the big picture and stayed focused on their tight deadline. As Gia opened her laptop, Golden asked her, "So what's your background, Gia? Do you have experience in large projects from the ground up?"

"Oh, yes! My dad is a contractor and I've been to so many jobsites with him that I can't even count. He does a lot of work for Mr. LeBaron."

"Who?" Golden asked.

"Ummm...Mr. LeBaron, our boss." Gia added with an eager look as if she were trying to spark a memory in Golden's mind.

"Oh yeah," Golden replied. "Sorry, I just have so much going on in my mind." Golden was happy for once that her complexion was so deep that Gia couldn't see the rush of hot blood flushing her face with embarrassment. *So, the lawyer's last name is LeBaron.* Golden made a mental note to research him later when she had time. Then she let out a large sigh. "Well, I'm happy you're here. We have a tight deadline." Gia nodded.

"So, have you seen the property yet?" Gia asked Golden.

Golden couldn't believe that she hadn't even thought of visiting the mansion before hiring people. "Not yet," Golden replied coolly. "I was waiting for you to get here so we could see it together," Golden lied.

Gia allowed a large smile to spread across her face. "Okay, well we can take the SUV out front that I arrived in. Mr. LeBaron let me know that will be our transportation for the next few months and we can use it for anything we need." The two gathered their laptops and purses and headed to the mansion.

Gia hopped in the driver seat and used the GPS that already had the mansion's address plugged in. Gia drove as Golden searched through the contents of her new laptop. She found a chart with all of the tasks needed to complete the mansion project. Gia glanced over to Golden's laptop. "Oh, good. I see LeBaron uploaded the chart that I proposed."

"You did this?" Golden looked at Gia, surprised.

"Yeah, I managed a few projects while working with my dad's company."

"So, you didn't learn this in college?"

"I learned some of the technical stuff and computer programs, but most of everything I learned is from my dad. Can't beat real-world experience." Gia added with a smile.

As the SUV started up the incline to the mansion, the top of it could be seen breaking through the skyline. As they pulled up to the front door, Golden's eyes grew wide with delight. She'd never seen a house so magnificent in architecture and style before. The front of the house featured ivy-colored stucco, accented with monochromatic bricks ranging from deep brown to tan. Golden hoped the brick accent was carried through the design in the rest of the house because she liked what she saw so far. As she admired the house, the large front cedar doors opened, and a middle-aged man in a long-sleeve white shirt paired with black slacks appeared. Gia leaned over to Golden. "That's Anselmo, he's the house manager and will help us with anything we need." Golden nodded, although she didn't know the duties of a house manager and didn't want to let Gia know.

Golden stepped out onto the circle driveway, noticing that it was painted to match the house; she nodded in approval and walked toward Anselmo's outstretched hand and warm smile.

"Greetings. I am Anselmo and will take you on a tour of the property. Please let me know if there is anything that is not up to your standards, and I will see to it immediately." Anselmo gave a genuine smile, curt bow, and then ushered the women inside.

They were greeted by marble flooring accented with a champagne pigment in the circular foyer. Their eyes immediately went toward the unique chandelier that coiled upward with what seemed like a thousand lights suspended mid-air, reaching to the second floor. There was a double staircase on either side of the circular staircase. Golden loved the clean look of the space and that the architect chose to use white marble to create the balusters and handrails. Anselmo carefully watched Golden and Gia's reactions as they took in the foyer. When their eyes naturally returned to him, he continued with the tour of the property. There was a library downstairs that Golden loved. She wanted this room to be a focal point for club members to get drinks and begin to unwind. She gave Gia notes to have the room repainted into hunter green with dark leather couches to achieve a sexy mood. Golden also wanted to mix up the lighting of the library, as well as that of the whole house. She wanted the club members to have the illusion of privacy; that way their inhibitions would lower faster, along with their wallets. Golden went through each bedroom, quickly giving Gia notes on which rooms would have the themes she already discussed with the lawyer. She still hadn't gotten used to thinking of him as LeBaron yet. Golden was impressed with the inside pool and sauna and thought it wise to wall off a small area by the indoor pool for a masseuse. There was an outdoor pool that was partially covered by the upstairs breezeway that separated one half of the mansion from the other. Golden decided to place a small poolside bar with an attendant underneath the covered breezeway. One thing she learned from working at Club V was to keep the alcohol flowing, and she planned to do that flawlessly. She wanted to create an experience that would have the club members coming back for more.

After touring the property and making notes, Golden suggested they go back to the office and start contacting florists, painters, contractors, liquor distributors, escorts, waitstaff, housekeepers, chefs, and any other people they may need to make Golden's dream mansion a reality.

Once back in the office, Golden ran through her checklist with Gia, making sure they added every portion of the project schedule to the spreadsheet that was already created on Golden's laptop.

"I'm happy you're here," Golden said and genuinely smiled at Gia.

Gia returned Golden's smile. "What was that for?"

"I just want you to know how much I appreciate you and that I couldn't have pulled this off without you, Gia." The two women exchanged smiles.

"Okay...let's get to work. So, we have five bedrooms and five themes. We have heaven and hell rooms, the psychedelic room, the Western room, and I was stuck on another room idea," Golden stated.

"What about a bondage room?" Gia asked in a low voice.

Golden swiveled her chair around to meet Gia's eyes and both girls burst into a fit of laughter. It was late in the evening at this point, and the girls were weary from their first day of work. They didn't even know why they were laughing or what made them continually laugh.

Gia broke the silence, saying, "You know, I could help design the room, Golden. I worked as a dom to help play for my last two years of college when my dad couldn't work because he got hurt on a job. I know what types of whips, chains, buckles, gags, swings, and pads to get."

"What you mean pads? Like knee pads or period pads?"

"No, silly, soundproof padding, so the screams can't he heard."

Golden pressed her lips together in a thin smile and slowly turned around to face her laptop. "Okay, Miss Thang, I see you." Golden let out a long yawn. It was already past midnight. "Oh Gia, you'd better get home, it's late, girl. And I think I'm about to call it a night anyways."

"Oh, Mr. LeBaron didn't tell you? I'm staying in a room here until the project's done. That way we can work nonstop."

"No, I didn't know that. Well, that's good." Golden added curtly. She was growing tired of feeling like she was the help and Gia knew more than her about her own damn project! As Golden walked to her room, she only got more infuriated because she felt like she was being manipulated from the start; even her friendship with Tatiana felt staged. Golden pushed the thought to the back of her mind. Tati was her real friend. *But is she*, Golden questioned?

The next day Golden and Gia were up right before sunrise making phone calls, setting up meetings, and making Golden's dream of a members-only escort mansion in Vegas a reality. The next week passed by so quickly that Golden barely slept. Gia noticed Golden sleeping at her desk one afternoon. She gently nudged Golden's shoulder and handed her a pill and a glass of water.

Golden woke, embarrassed. "Oh, I must've dozed off. I'm sorry, Gia."

"No worries. Here...take this, it will help give you energy and keep you awake."

Golden took the peach-colored pill without question. "Good, because I need a pick-me-up. It's only eleven and I'm over here knocked out at my desk."

Within about twenty minutes of taking the pill, Golden began to feel her concentration swell, and she had a surge of energy. It was nearing opening night, and everything was completely on schedule. Golden hired body paint artists for the first night, and she hired live models to walk around posing nude to get the club members relaxed. The escorts she hired were some of the most beautiful people she'd ever seen. Golden wholeheartedly believed in equal opportunity and made sure she had women and men who were sexually fluid and carefree while also putting their health and safety first. Golden wanted to be there to see how the guests responded to the ambience, so she decided to attend opening night and watch the night unfold from the security control room; then her contract would be fulfilled. She didn't want to watch people having sex, she only wanted their responses to the lighting, food, alcohol, ambience, room availability, and room turnover. Golden had a secret door installed in each room that connected to a hallway for waitstaff to clean the room and quickly prep it for the next guest.

Golden watched the security monitors, happy with what she saw. Then she received a phone call from the lawyer congratulating her on her accomplishment. He also told her to check her bank account. Golden was stunned! She'd never seen so much money in her account. The lawyer told her to take the night off and celebrate. Golden felt a surge of energy and knew she needed to dance it off. She was so jittery and excited that the security guard made note of her inability to sit still. She exclaimed that she was super excited to see her vision come to life. The security guard raised his eyebrow questioningly but decided against any further communication and got back to watching the club members, switching from one point of view to the next, ensuring safety and house-rule compliance.

Golden sat in her chair, staring at the happy club members, and she was so proud of her accomplishment. She picked up her phone to call Tatiana on video chat. "Hey, girl! Where you at, bitch? Let's celebrate!" Golden screamed into the phone.

"Hey, Golden, I'm really busy right now, but we can link up tomorrow, m'kay?" And Tatiana hung up the video call as quickly as she answered it. The security guard judgingly shook his head.

Golden decided to text her driver and go back to the house. The whole ride home, Golden kept fidgeting and looking out the window. She'd taken four of the "energy pills" that Gia gave her that day, and she couldn't sit still. She fixed her mind on talking to Grandmother and telling her about her success. Then, for the first time that day, Golden stopped fidgeting and thought about Grandmother. She wondered when the last time was she'd spoken to her. Golden couldn't quite recall their last conversation, so she called. She knew it was late and Grandmother was more than likely asleep, but in that moment, she had a nagging urge to hear her grandmother's voice. The phone range without answer. She pictured her grandmother hearing the phone and wondering who could be calling this late. Then she pictured her grandmother realizing it was probably her, and it would take a moment for her to get out of bed. Then she imagined her turning on her bedside table lamp, getting out of her bed, and turning on the lamp by the couch where the house phone was. Her grandmother was one of the only people Golden knew who had a house phone.

Golden opened her bag and grabbed one of her peach "energy pills," popped it into her mouth, and washed it down with a bottled water that was always on standby in the SUV cupholder. She sank into the leather seats and waited for the pill to take effect. She remembered the burst of energy she used to get from her pills; now she got jumpy and irritated if she went too long without them.

Golden awoke to the driver standing next to her with the door open. "Miss...Miss, we're here." Golden felt groggy and embarrassed that she'd fallen asleep and had to be woken up. She tiptoed through the front door to her room and shut her bedroom door quietly. She thought to herself that it was time she bought her own place in Vegas; she was sick of sneaking around in an attempt to avoid G and Tatiana.

Golden glanced at her phone and decided she had enough time to quickly jump in the shower, go to bed, and call Grandmother in the morning. As Golden showered, her thoughts drifted to Grandmother's Sunday cooking. It was Saturday night, and she knew Grandmother was preparing her meal for Sunday. Maybe it was a roast, baked chicken with herbs, or a meatloaf. *Mmmm...that sounds so good*, Golden thought. And with some fresh mashed potatoes and her grandmother's famous gravy! Golden's mouth began to water as she stepped out of the shower and dried off.

Golden looked in the mirror and noticed how tired she looked: her eyes a dull, pale green and hallow underneath. She thought about the last few months of hard work she'd put in and imagined all the debauchery that was currently taking place at the mansion. She looked at the mirror, then glanced away, her own thoughts making her blush.

Golden pulled on her favorite night shirt, climbed into bed, and grabbed her cellphone to call Grandmother once more before she went to bed. She dialed the number and the phone rang two times before it picked up.

"Hey, Grandmother."

The line was silent. Golden repeated, "Grandmother?"

"Golden." It was Althea's voice on the other end. "She gone." Althea said slowly. Golden heard what Althea said but couldn't process the words, or their meaning, because Golden was stuck on Althea calling Golden by her first name, which she rarely did. Althea usually referred to Golden as "little girl." Golden's name sounded so unnatural on Althea's lips. There was a long silence and neither of them interrupted.

Then, Althea, unable to hold back any longer, burst into breathless sobs. Golden was confused, trying to process Althea's tears and her calling Golden's name. Althea then began wailing loudly, causing the phone to vibrate Golden's eardrum. Golden quickly removed the phone from her ear as tears began to flow down her own face. Golden heard the phone drop and then a short pause. Golden listened intently; she needed answers. She heard fumbling, then a familiar voice,

"Golden, is that you? You better come home, Golden. Golden, are you there?" Golden recognized the voice at once: it was Marquez.

Golden didn't respond. She was still processing that her grandmother died.

"I said you need to come home. Your grandmother is gone," Marquez said in a gentle voice that only he knew how to use with Golden to calm and center her.

Golden drew in a sharp breath, realizing she'd hadn't taken one since Althea was on the phone. Golden quickly blinked her eyes. There were so many tears that she couldn't see, so she just closed them. "Wh...wha...what happened?" Golden stammered.

Marquez took and deep breath, let it out, and began. "She had a stroke, Golden. Your mom was..." he hesitated. "Away." He took another deep breath and continued. "When she got back, she found her. It had been about four days." Golden heard Marquez catch a sob in his throat. "I'm sorry, Golden, I should've known. I should've went over and checked on her. I..." His voice trailed off. There was nothing left to say.

"I'm on my way," Golden said flatly and ended the phone call. *Grandmother dead? But how?* she thought. *How could this be? And where the fuck was my momma? Probably out fucking, getting drunk, or passed out somewhere with some dude.* Golden's thoughts were racing as she roughly grabbed her suitcases and began packing. She kept stopping to cry, bending over, clutching her own waist, trying keep her soul from leaving her belly as she cried the hardest she'd ever cried in her life. Golden sent a text to her driver and let him know she needed a ride to the airport. Golden figured she would book a flight when she got to the ticket counter.

The ride to the airport was torture. Golden thought that there was a mistake. She ran through the possibilities of how someone could mistake her grandmother for dead. *Maybe she's just in a deep sleep or a coma*, Golden thought. *Maybe she's still in the hospital.* Golden now wished she'd asked more questions when talking to Marquez. She knew she would be there soon, so she tried to keep her head from swirling with unanswered questions.

CHAPTER NINETEEN

HOMEGOING

Golden arrived at her hometown airport. She'd forgotten how tiny everything was here compared to the city of Vegas. She waited at the baggage claim, battered and emotionally weathered from her two connecting flights and four-hour layover. She grabbed her bags and headed outside, looking for her driver. She shook her head, remembering she was in her small Midwestern town and that her Vegas driver was not outside waiting for her. Golden started to open an app on her phone when an old yellow cab pulled up in front of her. The driver asked where she was going and if she needed a ride.

She hesitantly climbed in. It was almost five a.m. and she knew no one would be up on any ride share apps this early. The cab driver graciously helped her with her bags, eying her the whole time. Golden was grateful the cab driver wasn't talkative because she needed every moment to prepare to walk into her childhood home to face her mother in Grandmother's absence.

Golden's head was pounding by the time the cab pulled in front of her home. Her stomach let out a loud grumble as she grabbed her bags out of the trunk. She could barely lift them because she was so weak. Golden tried to remember her last meal, but her memory was blank. The last thing she remembered was being at the ticket counter. The cab drove off and Golden stood outside with her bags, staring at the front steps; there were only four, but Golden felt like there were hundreds. *One foot in front of the other*, Golden thought as she started up the steps. She made it to the last step, a sinking feeling in the pit of her stomach.

As Golden climbed each step, she thought about how Marquez and Althea must have made a mistake. Her grandmother couldn't be dead. Golden hadn't shared her success at the mansion with her. She hadn't told Grandmother about LeBaron and Gia, or Tatiana's shady actions. She wanted to see the pride in her grandmother's eyes when Golden described her designs. Golden's grandmother was the only person who encouraged Golden's passions. If it weren't for her grandmother, Golden would've never believed it was possible that anyone would want her designs, much less her input about designing. She made it to the top step and reached out to open the screen door, but it was locked. *Damn it*, Golden thought.

Golden started banging on the screen door. She knew that if it was locked, then Althea was inside. She hadn't thought about dealing with Althea tonight. There was no way to anticipate what type of mood Althea was going to be in, so Golden rolled her shoulders back as if putting on armor to defend against her mother's verbal onslaughts.

She heard rumbling around inside the house, then heavy footsteps making their way to the front door. Golden saw Althea fingers bend the blinds to peek through. "It's me...Golden." There was a small pause, then the locks unbolted one by one.

The front door swung open, revealing a tattered-looking Althea. Her hair was in a ratted mess on top of her head. Her eye makeup was smudged under her eyes and the remnants of a red lipstick stained her dry, cracked lips. When Althea swung open the door, a smoke-filled haze hit Golden so strongly that her nose burned.

"I see you finally brought yo' ass back, huh?" Althea snorted at Golden.

"Can you please let me in? Open the door." Golden softly pleaded with Althea. She didn't know what frame of mind her mother was in, so she didn't want to push her. Plus, Golden was so tired from her travels, she didn't think she had the energy to argue, even if Althea provoked an argument. "I been flying all day," Golden added.

"Oh! You tired! You tired?" Althea began shouting.

Golden knew that coming here was a mistake.

"I'm the one that found her!" Althea screamed at Golden through the screen door. "Not you! Me!"

Althea walked away from the door to get her lit cigarette resting in the ashtray on the coffee table. She aggressively grabbed the cigarette and took a large pull, filling her entire lungs. Then she walked back to the screen door, unlocked it, and blew the smoke in Golden's face as she opened the door. Golden involuntarily choked on the smoke. Althea, seemingly please, stomped off and shoved herself into the center of the couch. She popped her cigarette in the vicinity of the ashtray as Golden hesitantly walked inside.

Golden quickly surveyed the room. She couldn't smell or feel Grandmother's warm presence, nor could she smell her cooking. She half-expected to look into the kitchen and see her grandmother standing over the stove in her favorite red-checkered robe. But all Golden could see was a mismatch of bowls covered in foil and plastic wrap. Golden's eyes then went to each corner of the room where there was trash and debris and muddy footsteps on the carpet. She stared in disbelief. She'd never seen her childhood home so filthy. Golden's eyes didn't know where to focus; they shifted back and forth from Althea to the house.

"Well, I came home to help plan the services." Golden said matter-of-factly. She didn't want to cause another argument with Althea, but she knew Grandmother's wishes and how she wanted her home-going service to go. Golden's grandmother told her who she wanted to preach and the food she wanted cooked and by whom. She even told Golden which funeral home she wanted to use. Her grandmother had it all planned out.

"Services? What services you talking 'bout? She right over there in the corner." Althea's head motioned to a side table sitting in the far corner of the living room. Golden shakily walked toward a cardboard box that had the words *Mary Rose* written on it.

Golden quickly whipped around, and in two giant leaps, she was across the room, choking Althea from behind. Althea was no match for Golden; as she struggled to stand, Golden pushed her further down into the couch. As Golden took a split second to readjust her grip, Althea jerked her elbow back, landing a blow to Golden's cheek.

"Bitch!" Golden yelled as she grabbed her cheek that now had a small cut from the blow. Althea scrambled to her feet and crouched down in front of the couch, ready to pounce on Golden.

"What the fuck is wrong with ya'll?" A voice boomed from the side of the ravenous pair. Althea and Golden moved only their eyes to the door and saw to whom the voice belonged. "Are ya'll fucking crazy?" Marquez was asking a genuine question. "Golden, yo grandmamma just died and now you in here fightin' yo' momma? What the fuck?"

The two were heaving, breathless, looking at each other, as if for the first time. They both stood up straight, Golden wiping her eye and Althea retying her robe.

Golden turned toward Marquez. "She had my fucking Grandmother cremated?" Golden yelled. "Her shit was already paid for, that's why I got here so fast. Because I knew what she wanted."

Then Golden set her eyes on Althea and a hatred she never felt before flooded her entire body. Golden knew Althea was jealous of her and Grandmother's relationship, but she never thought Althea would cremate her. And cremate her before talking to Golden about it.

"Well, that shit was cheaper." Althea spit out.

And in that instant, Golden lunged at Althea again, but Althea was ready and quickly evaded Golden's grasp.

"You two, fucking stop!" Marquez's voice boomed and echoed, seemingly in every room of the house.

"Look, Golden, I know you and your grandmother were close. But we tried to get in contact with you for damn near a week with no answer. I even went to Club V to get your homegirl's number. Called her and she said she hadn't talked to you. So, yo' momma did what she thought was best. And she did it alone."

Golden looked at Althea and fresh tears were streaming down her face. "I know you loved her, but I loved her too!" Althea sobbed, "I loved her first."

Marquez walked over to Althea who fell apart in his arms as he softly guided her to the couch. Golden felt weak and defeated, and she backed up, collapsing in an armchair against the wall.

Marquez made sure Althea was alright. Then he got up, lifted Golden's bags, and carried them into her room. He came back, gathering Golden, and ushered her to bed. "You had a long day. Imma stay here while you get some rest."

Golden was too tired to argue and welcomed the company. When Golden awoke the next morning, Marquez was gone. She got up to use the bathroom. She cried, for what seemed like hours, sitting on the toilet while thoughts of her grandmother being dead sank in. She gathered the strength to move from the bathroom back to her bed. Marquez's words from the night before, about talking to her homegirl, kept playing in her head. Her head was pounding so hard she couldn't think logically. She needed relief.

Golden shuffled into the kitchen, looking for pain relievers. She noticed Althea's bedroom door was open and she wasn't on the couch. Golden was relieved she had the house to herself. She needed a moment to think. She looked inside the bowls on the table that had started to spoil, and she decided to clean up. She didn't have the mental strength for anything more complex than that. Golden finally felt like showering, allowing the water to wash away her tears. She couldn't stop crying. Every breath she took triggered a tear and reminded her of the breaths her grandmother no longer had.

Golden, exhausted, fell asleep again and woke to the sun setting. She heard her phone vibrate and ignored it. Her phone had been going off since before she left Vegas. Phone calls, texts, and emails from everyone she was in charge of at the mansion. That life seemed so far away right then. *Almost a memory,* Golden thought. She put her phone on the charger and decided to go outside for fresh air, away from the scent of stale cigarettes and wasted liquor.

Golden sat on the front steps of her porch, bent forward with her head resting on her hands. She heard the sound of gravel beneath feet approaching her. Golden barely had the strength to lift her head. It was Marquez, standing tall, chiseled, and chocolate. *Why couldn't I love this man?* Golden asked herself as he approached.

"Hey, I see you up and about. How you feeling?"

"Okay...I guess," Golden replied hesitantly. But that was a lie; she was far from fine. Every breath she took, she felt like she was stealing it.

"You and your mom gotta do better. Ya'll all ya'll got," Marquez stated the obvious. Golden did not meet his gaze. Marquez sat next to Golden on the steps, just like he did when they would talk late nights about their future and what they wanted to be when they moved out of their hometown.

They sat in silence for about ten minutes. Golden always loved that Marquez didn't feel the need to talk unnecessarily, and she could just enjoy the quiet with him.

"So, what was you doin' all that time out in Vegas?" Marquez asked.

"Don't even matter no more," Golden replied, looking off into the distance at nothing in particular.

"You going back?"

"I don't know what I'm gonna do. I may stay here to keep an eye on my mom, but I don't think that will work out in the long run. I wanna go somewhere I choose. Don't know where that is yet though," Golden replied, biting the inside of her lip.

"Enough about me. What you been up to since I been gone?"

Marquez laughed. "Well...I opened my own auto shop." Then a huge grin covered his face.

"Whaaat! Get the fuck outta here! You always said that's what you wanted to do, Quez. I'm proud of you. Look at us living out our dreams." Golden's voice trailed off thinking about the huge opportunity she left behind in Vegas.

"What you mean?" Marquez asked.

"Damn, you don't miss shit, huh?" Golden playfully bumped into Marquez. "Well, while I was in Vegas, long story short, my girl Tatiana introduced me to some heavy hitters, and I did a whole concept design for their business. Head to toe! Everything from outfits to hiring people, creating a whole experience." Golden stopped mid-sentence, closing her eyes and bending her face skyward to soak up the sunshine. Then she stopped, feeling eyes on her.

Marquez was staring at her with a soft smile playing on his lips.

"What, Quez? Why you lookin' at me like that?"

"Cuz I ain't never heard you talk about nothing like that before. Really sounds like you found your dreams in Vegas," Marquez said, confirming Golden's feelings she had never taken the time to process.

"Yeah, but that job is over with. I'm basically done, and I've been paid for it. I was thinking about asking for another project to work on, but then..." her voice trailed off.

"Well, you got experience now, and you one of the smartest, most talented girls I know, Goldie. You can do that shit...like whatever you wanna do. You always have." Marquez and Golden's grandmother were always her biggest supporters.

Golden hooked her arm inside of Marquez's. "So, tell me...what these hoes out here looking like? You better keep yo' eye out now, especially now you got yo own business. You likin' anyone out here?" Golden asked optimistically.

"Naw, you know there's only one girl for me." Marquez let his statement linger in the air.

CHAPTER TWENTY

CIRCLES

A few days passed, and Golden was coming to grips with the passing of her grandmother. She decided to go and sit inside her grandmother's room to feel her presence again. "Hey, Grandmother," Golden said out loud, sitting on her grandmother's bed. She looked around the room, her finger trailing on the dresser, books, and bedposts of her grandmother's bed. Golden's eyes stopped to rest on her favorite picture of her mom and dad and herself around the age of three. Both of her parents stood smiling back at her, each one holding her hand. Althea looked so fly! Her hair was cut in an asymmetrical bob and she wore gold-bamboo earrings, a ring on every finger, and a large herringbone chain to set off her look. Her dad was dressed more low-key, but he was still dappered-down in a designer sweater with the sleeves pushed up and dark denim pants to match. The only sign of wealth was his Rolex on his left wrist. Behind them was her dad's favorite car: his all-black '98 Acura Legend. *Damn, they looked so happy,* Golden thought.

She sat on the bedspread and deflated into a heap, resting her head on her grandmother's pillows. She sat up because she felt something hard under the pillowcase. Golden felt inside the pillowcase and retrieved a small, black book. She thumbed through the book, instantly recognizing her grandmother's handwriting. Golden quickly closed the book, feeling as if she were violating her grandmother's private thoughts.

Golden bit her lip, holding her grandmother's diary. Golden had so many unanswered questions: Were her final thoughts written down; Did she know she was dying; Was she proud of Golden? So many questions swirled around in Golden's head. She repositioned herself on the bed and resigned to reading only the last entry of the diary. The entry was dated three weeks before her grandmother passed.

Talked to baby girl today. She sounds happy. I know that she's on her way to greatness. God, I pray you remove every obstacle in her way, even herself. Amen.

Golden slammed the diary shut and started lightly sobbing. She held her grandmother's diary close to her chest, rocking back and forth and sobbing. *She was really proud of me,* Golden kept repeating to herself. *She was really proud of me.* The thought repeated in her mind, and the tears continued falling while she sobbed and eventually rocked herself to sleep.

Golden awoke in her grandmother's room, realizing it was nightfall. She'd cried herself to sleep for the millionth time, it seemed. She still couldn't understand how her grandmother died or why Althea cremated her so quickly, knowing how close Golden and her grandmother were. She was furious with Althea for not trying to contact Golden.

"I never even got to say goodbye," Golden whispered to herself while still gripping tightly her grandmother's journal. Golden's thoughts were interrupted by a faint knock at the front door. She didn't move to answer the knock. She didn't care who it was. Golden envisioned one of the church members dropping off another flavorless, mushy, or overly salty dish. She was tired of getting pathetic stares whenever she left the house or receiving the *Sorry for your loss* text messages. The knocking continued to grow louder, gaining in urgency. Golden remained in her grandmother's bed, too exhausted to move. She heard a rustling of movement coming from Althea's room at the end of the hallway. The knocking continued.

Then she heard heavy footsteps marching from Althea's room to the front door, flooding the quiet of the house. "Who is it?" Althea yelled from inside the closed door. Golden strained to hear the response. "Who?" Althea questioned. Then more silence.

Then Golden heard the front door swing open and hit the wall. The door's blinds followed, slamming against the wall with force. Golden bolted upright in her grandmother's bed and made her way to the living room. She feared for the safety of whoever was on the other side of that door. Golden stopped mid-step as she saw who was at the door. She took a half step back with her mouth open in shock.

"What the fuck you want?" Althea spat with all the anger and venom she could muster. "What the fuck you doin' here, LeBaron?"

Golden's head snapped back. *LeBaron,* she thought, "Umm, how you know my boss?" Golden questioned Althea.

"Yo' boss? What the fuck you mean, 'yo' boss'?"

"I was just checking on her...on Golden," LeBaron stammered.

"What the fuck you checkin' on my motherfuckin' child for? You never gave a damn about her before." Althea was shouting through the locked screen door. Then Althea turned to Golden. "And you know him?"

LeBaron's eyes shifted from Golden to Althea, panicked that he said the wrong thing.

Golden slowly approached the door, but before she could get closer, Althea slammed the door and swung around to face Golden in the same swift move.

"Yeah, I met him in Vegas. He's my boss," Golden replied.

Althea quickly opened the door and unlocked the screen door, almost hitting LeBaron.

"You dirty motherfucker!" Althea yelled at LeBaron.

"Wait, Ma! You know him?" Golden yelled at Althea's back. She needed answers.

"Look, Thea, I know I bounced after Diamond died," LeBaron started. Althea was taken off guard. It had been so long since she heard Diamond's name. "But we had a plan, Thea. Diamond had a plan. I didn't wanna leave, but we had a plan. You know that Diamond was the brains, and I was the muscle. But he told me that if anything ever happened to him..." LeBaron's voice trailed off and large tears started to drop from his eyes as his voice broke. "If anything happened to him," he continued, "I was supposed to get out of town, start new, and leave the game behind."

"But you left us!" Althea pleaded and pointed to her and Golden. "You left when we needed you most."

"I know. I'm sorry, Thea, but you gotta understand, I was just following orders." Lebaron tried wiping the tears from his eyes.

"So, you knew my dad?" Golden spoke up.

"Yeah, I did. We hustled together. He was my brother. I loved him." LeBaron added quietly.

"So why me, why now? Are you on some sick-ass shit? I don't know what the fuck's going on." Golden threw her hands up and paced the living room. She didn't know who or what to believe. She was faced with a man who said he knew her father but acted like he was her boss for months, never mentioning his true identity.

"Please, just let me explain to both of you," LeBaron pleaded. "Let me explain, then I will be out of both of your lives forever."

Golden looked at Althea's face and saw the same pain and distrust she felt. How could they trust this man? But what choice did they have if they wanted the truth to a twenty-one-year-old mystery. Althea's and Golden's silences signaled to LeBaron to continue with his story.

"Like I was saying, before D died, he had me set up a trust for you, Golden, that matured on your twenty-fifth birthday. The money I paid you was from your trust." LeBaron looked from Althea to Golden to make sure they were still following his story. "Golden, your dad loved you more than anything, and he wanted to make sure you had a future." Then he looked at Althea. "Thea, he knew how much you loved him, but he also knew that you were young at the time and Mother Rose was a damn criminal and if she knew you had any money, then she was gonna blow through it. So, he set up another account for Grandmother. She always had access to money."

LeBaron paused again so Golden and Althea could process his words.

"So, my grandmother knew about you the whole time?" Golden asked, still stunned by the story LeBaron was telling them.

"Yeah, she knew. And she made sure you had everything you needed, from art supplies to sewing kits. She was so proud of you, Golden." LeBaron said in a soft voice that was convincing, which made Golden's demeanor soften.

"How you know she was proud of me?" Golden asked sheepishly.

"I talked to her every now and then over the years, and she would keep me updated on the two of you. But Diamond was clear, I was never to intervene until you turned twenty-five and your trust matured. So, I spent the years trying to be a better version of myself. I used our drug money to pay for school. It wasn't easy because I was a high school dropout, but I knew I had to get out the game if I didn't wanna end up..." LeBaron's voice trailed off.

"So, then your grandmother told me she thought you were on the wrong path and losing confidence in yourself, so I set you up to meet Tatiana."

Golden's eyes flashed at LeBaron.

"Hold on, Golden. I only sent her here to offer you a job as a makeup artist and stylist, but you two became friends and she took a liking to you. Then you started stripping. I told Tatiana to bring you to Vegas and she was never to see you again because of the bullshit she pulled."

Golden quizzically looked at LeBaron. "What bullshit did she pull, exactly?"

"She was gonna try and set you up with her pimp, G. He's a low-level leech that does some odd jobs for me. But I threatened to kill 'em both if they ever so much as uttered another word to you, Golden." LeBaron's facial expression cooled and Golden saw the reserved man she was initially introduced to in their first meeting.

Golden sat, placing her head in her hands on the couch cushion next to Althea. It was so much to process. Her grandmother was keeping this secret all this time. Her dad had a trust fund set up for her and LeBaron, the lawyer, was his right-hand man. Golden shook her head as a stress headache began to form.

"Look, I just came here because I thought it was time you both," LeBaron looked from Althea to Golden, "knew the truth."

"Well, I want my fucking cut!" Althea stood, facing LeBaron.

"Thea, there is no real money for you. You can have the remainder of what's in Grandmother's bank accounts and a monthly stipend, but that's it," LeBaron said coolly to Althea. She knew better than to argue with LeBaron; she knew the man he once was and that was enough for her. Twenty-one years wasn't a long enough break for her to try LeBaron. What he said was law.

LeBaron turned to Golden. "Look, Golden, I came here to give you a life changing opportunity like your dad offered me. Without him, I wouldn't be the man I am today."

Golden listened intently to LeBaron. "I've arranged for you to go to a fashion school in Atlanta. It's high-tech and reputable. I already had Gia apply for you and you've been accepted. Classes start in a few weeks. It's up to you what you want to do with your future. Either way, you'll have your trust. I'll have Gia contact you tomorrow and you can go over all the details. I'm so sorry for misleading you."

"Why didn't you just tell me who you were? That you knew my dad?" Golden asked.

"Because some things are better left unsaid. And you already had a dad. I am no replacement, never tried to be," LeBaron said as he turned for the door to leave.

"LeBaron, thank you," Golden called after him. He nodded and left.

Chapter Twenty-One

ASCENSION

Gia contacted Golden the next day, giving her all the details of her new school. Golden was still unsure about what she was going to do. LeBaron left Golden's laptop for her before he left so she had all the school documents that Gia had submitted on her behalf. Golden felt slightly grateful to have something to briefly pause the grief of her grandmother. She started to recall all the conversations about fashion school between Grandmother and herself. Golden always dreamed of going but never had the courage to apply. Now the opportunity was within her grasp, but she doubted her worthiness.

Golden was sitting outside, looking at the fashion school's online brochure, when she saw Marquez pull up outside of his house. Noticing Golden, he crossed the street. Marquez sat next to Golden with the familiar smell of oil and car engines on his clothing. Golden found the smell surprisingly comforting. "So, what's up? You decided what you gonna do yet?" Marquez always got to the point; he never minced words.

"I don't know," Golden replied as she continued to scroll the website. Marquez politely grabbed her laptop and closed it. "Talk to me."

Golden sighed. "I don't know. It's like...it's like I didn't even earn it. I got in because LeBaron pulled some strings for me."

"Okay, so...and? What's the problem? It' no different than other privileged kids getting into college because of who their parents are. I mean, shit, you still gotta do the work right?" Marquez stared at Golden waiting for an answer. "Right?" He repeated.

"Yeah, I guess you right. Just never thought about it like that before." The two sat in silence for a moment longer.

"Well, I'm gonna get outta here so I can shower and check on Momma. But let me ask you this, G. What you gonna do if you stay here? Huh? Live with yo' momma? Work back at Club V? The mall? I mean...you really got a chance, Goldie. You can be who you always talked about being. Man, if I was you, I would go for it. Fuck how you got it, just get it." Marquez turned to leave.

Golden sat on the porch until the sun went down, envisioning herself at fashion school. She wondered what it would be like. What would she learn? She browsed the course descriptions again and a smile started playing across her lips. The descriptions were the exact types of things Golden wanted to learn. She closed her laptop and went inside. *Here goes nothing,* she thought.

Two weeks later, Golden found herself at the footsteps of her new fashion school. She stood outside, nervous and hesitant. She didn't know what awaited at the top of those steps, but she knew what awaited her at the bottom. Golden briefly looked up to the sky. "Grandmother...Daddy...this one's for ya'll." Then she put one foot in front of the other and climbed the stairs to her new future.

Chapter Twenty-Two

About the Author

Kenya Stemmons is the author of *GoldenRose*, which is her fiction debut. She is a proud mother of two wonderfulchildren who are her reason for carving out a literary career. She was born andraised in Springfield, IL where most of her stories take place. She an alumnusof Southern Illinois University in Edwardsville where she received her Bachelorof Science in Business Administration and the University of IllinoisSpringfield where she received her Master of Public Administration. Kenya'smidwestern upbringing is woven throughout her stories and she is honored tocall Illinois her home state.

Her earlyupbringing spurred her love of literature by roaming the endless stacks ofbooks in her local library. Every summer she prided herself on reading booksthat stimulated her mind and expanded her world. her favorite books to read in heryouth were biographies and fiction novels ranging from fantasy to literaturefeaturing African American characters. She also loved reading aboutentrepreneurship and seeing the stories of black people thriving in their businessthrough the pages of *Black Enterprise Magazine* back in the late 1990's.

During theCOVID-19 pandemic, Kenya began thinking about an idea for writing her ownnovel. She started to sketch an outline for her characters and the storylinematerialized before her very eyes. After writing a few pages of her firstnovel, the page count grew into an entire novel.

The Virgo inher wanted to make sure she was "doing everything right," and respecting thecraft of writing; so, she enrolled herself in some online writing courses toensure her work was worth people's money. She understands that everyone has achoice where to spend their money and wanted to produce the type of writingthat is worth people's time and money.

She took herwriting journey a step further and wanted to be around like-minded individuals,so she decided to join the Atlanta's Writer's Club. The experience with theAtlanta's Writer's Club afforded her the opportunity to interact with otherpublished authors and aspiring authors. The Atlanta's Writer's Club also offersa safe haven for when that all dreaded imposter syndrome tries to rear its uglyhead.

She can now proudlylabel herself as a published author, but she didn't do it alone. A specialthank you is given to her children, sister, friends and family who encouraged herwhen the new ideas wouldn't come for the next chapter. Special recognition isalso given to her therapist and spiritual advisor who kept a stern hand on herto get *Golden Rose* completed. She is eternally grateful.